"What Accident?" The Words Were Out Before Raina Could Think.

"It was no big deal," Lucian protested.

Yes, yes it is a big deal. Raina's mind raced. A very big deal.

"What happened?"

He shook his head. "No idea."

"You mean—" she hesitated "—you don't remember? Nothing at all? Not even the wedding?" It was all she could do not to grab him by the shoulders and shake him.

"Nothing about the wedding, but everyone tells me that I had a great time."

Oh, you had a great time, all right, Raina thought. And not just at the wedding. "What's the last thing you *do* remember?" she asked curiously.

"Driving home after picking up my tux," Lucian said.

So he didn't remember her. Didn't remember meeting her, dancing with her, *making love with her all night....*

Dear Reader,

Welcome to Silhouette Desire, where every month you can count on finding six passionate, powerful and provocative romances.

The fabulous Dixie Browning brings us November's MAN OF THE MONTH, *Rocky and the Senator's Daughter,* in which a heroine on the verge of scandal arouses the protective *and* sensual instincts of a man who knew her as a teenager. Then Leanne Banks launches her exciting Desire miniseries, THE ROYAL DUMONTS, with *Royal Dad,* the timeless story of a prince who falls in love with his son's American tutor.

The Bachelorette, Kate Little's lively contribution to our 20 AMBER COURT miniseries, features a wealthy businessman who buys a date with a "plain Jane" at a charity auction. The intriguing miniseries SECRETS! continues with *Sinclair's Surprise Baby,* Barbara McCauley's tale of a rugged bachelor with amnesia who's stunned to learn he's the father of a love child.

In *Luke's Promise* by Eileen Wilks, we meet the second TALL, DARK & ELIGIBLE brother, a gorgeous rancher who tries to respect his wife-of-convenience's virtue, while *she* looks to *him* for lessons in lovemaking! And, finally, in Gail Dayton's delightful *Hide-and-Sheikh,* a lovely security specialist and a sexy sheikh play a game in which both lose their hearts…and win a future together.

So treat yourself to all six of these not-to-be-missed stories. You deserve the pleasure!

Enjoy,

Joan Marlow Golan

Joan Marlow Golan
Senior Editor, Silhouette Desire

Please address questions and book requests to:
Silhouette Reader Service
U.S.: 3010 Walden Ave., P.O. Box 1325, Buffalo, NY 14269
Canadian: P.O. Box 609, Fort Erie, Ont. L2A 5X3

Sinclair's
Surprise Baby
BARBARA McCAULEY

Published by Silhouette Books
America's Publisher of Contemporary Romance

SILHOUETTE BOOKS

ISBN 0-373-76402-2

SINCLAIR'S SURPRISE BABY

Copyright © 2001 by Barbara Joel

This edition published by arrangement with Harlequin Books S.A.

Visit Silhouette at www.eHarlequin.com

Printed in U.S.A.

BARBARA McCAULEY

lives in Southern California with her own handsome hero husband, Frank, who makes it easy to believe in and write about the magic of romance. With over twenty books written for Silhouette, Ms. McCauley has won and been nominated for numerous awards, including the prestigious RITA Award from the Romance Writers of America, Best Desire of the Year from *Romantic Times Magazine* and Best Short Contemporary from the National Readers' Choice Awards.

To Jo Leigh and Debbi Rawlins—
you guys are the best!

Prologue

Lucian Sinclair did not believe in love at first sight.

Like at first sight, sure.

Lust, most definitely.

But *love?* Absolutely not.

Love, if it truly existed at all, came with words like *commitment* and *forever* and *marriage.* Sort of like a suit, he decided. A suit that seemed to fit the rest of his family just fine, but on him, Lucian knew, the cut was way too tight, the design simply not his style. He was happy with his life exactly as it was. Single, uncomplicated, free to come and go as he pleased.

He intended to keep it that way.

He silently laughed at the unusual direction his thoughts had taken, then slipped quietly from the four-poster bed, careful not to disturb the woman sleeping so peacefully beside him. He knew she had a plane to catch in less than four hours and, since she'd had so little sleep last night, he thought it best not to wake her.

But then, he thought with a smile, he hadn't had much sleep last night, either.

Raina Sarbanes—he stood by the bed and looked down at her—had to be the most beautiful woman he'd ever seen.

Last night at Gabe and Melanie's wedding reception, he'd heard his new sister-in-law mention that her maid of honor had graced the cover of several fashion magazines before she'd started her own business three years ago as a clothing designer. He'd also heard she'd been married briefly to a Greek shipping tycoon six years ago, when she was twenty-two, that she'd studied design in New York and she was leaving tomorrow morning to work with a top designer in Italy.

But most of that he'd heard secondhand, from Melanie. Raina hadn't seemed to want to talk about herself, so over the course of the night they'd discussed a variety of safe subjects: Gabe and Melanie, Kevin, Melanie's son from a previous marriage, Lucian's construction business, the design school Raina had gone to in Italy. The fact that neither one of them was interested in a relationship at the moment.

Though brief, that discussion had been an important one. They'd both agreed that, while they were obviously extremely attracted to each other, they weren't looking for commitment or marriage.

But no conversation between them had been long or detailed. A kiss or a touch would quickly end whatever discussion they had been having. And then they would be in each other's arms once again, breathless, eager. *Hungry.*

He glanced down at her, fascinated by the way the early-morning light streamed softly through the lacy bedroom window and lit her stunning face. Unable to resist, he reached out and touched a strand of hair the color of dark, rich chocolate. Long, thick, glossy hair that flowed over a man's skin like a river of liquid silk—a river a man could easily dive into, then let himself be swept away.

The face that glorious hair framed was heart shaped, her smooth skin porcelain pale over high cheekbones and a straight nose. Her mouth was wide, her lips curved and full. Seductive. Enticing. And though her eyes were closed peacefully now, he knew they were blue. Startling blue, fringed by thick, dark lashes and delicately arched brows. It had been those eyes that had made his breath catch in his throat when he'd first met her at his brother's rehearsal dinner only two days ago.

He'd wanted her that quickly, with a desperation that had knocked the wind out of him. And to be honest, scared the hell out of him, as well. Never had a woman so completely disarmed him.

For that reason he'd kept his distance from her the past two days. Not that she'd given him any encouragement. If anything, he'd thought Raina had been indifferent to him, if not downright cold. Even his brothers had teased him that Melanie's best friend obviously had brains as well as looks, since she'd appeared to be immune to Lucian's dark, dangerous looks, which most women seemed so drawn to.

Then he'd offered to drive Raina back to Melanie

and Gabe's house after the wedding. In the blink of an eye everything had changed.

He was still a little confused as to who exactly had made the first move. All he knew was that once they'd stepped into the house, out of the softly falling snow, once they were alone, she was suddenly in his arms, her mouth hot and urgent under his. They barely made it to the bed before he was inside her, both of them gasping at the intensity of the need that consumed them. And when they managed to finally shed their clothes, the need had still been as strong, as powerful.

Was still there, he realized as he stared down at her.

He'd experienced lust before. Hell, at thirty-three, he'd certainly been no monk. But last night had been something different. Something indefinable. Something that went way beyond your average run-of-the-mill mutual attraction.

He wondered if maybe, just maybe, she might consider staying a few more days. With Gabe and Melanie gone on their honeymoon, he and Raina could have the house to themselves. Not that he was looking for anything beyond that, he told himself. Of course he wasn't.

But a few days, he thought. There was nothing permanent about that. He'd love to show her some of the Pennsylvania countryside, maybe take her to the five-acre lot he'd bought outside of town where he was framing the house he planned to live in one day.

He just wasn't quite ready to let her go.

He'd ask her with flowers, he decided. He wasn't sure where he'd find a bouquet at six-thirty in the morning, but he knew that Sydney Taylor, the woman his brother was head over heels in love with, always kept roses in her restaurant. He hated to wake Sydney up so early, but he was desperate.

He dressed quietly, found a piece of paper in the bedside table and left Raina a note on the pillow beside hers. "Be back in fifteen. Please don't leave. Lucian."

He grabbed his jacket and crept quietly from the bedroom. Outside, he drew the crisp winter air into his lungs, noted the icicles that had formed on the eaves overnight and the white mounds of fresh snow on the ground.

A perfect morning, he thought, then headed for his truck. He couldn't wait to get back.

Several minutes later, with a smile on her lips, the sleeping woman stirred. Her arm moved restlessly over the now-empty pillow beside hers.

Lucian's note slipped soundlessly between the antique headboard and the mattress.

At the exact same time, with his mind on Raina and anxious to get back, Lucian missed the patch of ice at Jordan's Junction. His truck fishtailed, then skidded off the road, and his world went black.

One

The town of Bloomfield County came alive in spring. Winter-naked trees sprouted new leaves. Brown, barren pastures turned lush green. Cherry blossoms scented the still-crisp air. It was a time for the earth to stir, to stretch and awaken to the warm sun. A time for beginnings.

A time for babies.

Just this afternoon, on the drive over to his brother Gabe's house, Lucian had spotted a dozen or so new calves at the Johnson farm and at least five new colts at the Bainbridge ranch. And yesterday, nestled under the front porch of the house he was building a few miles outside of town, he had discovered a litter of kittens. Six little balls of fur that hadn't even opened their eyes yet, mewing for their mama, a pretty orange tabby who watched anxiously from the edge of the nearby woods. Lucian had sweet-talked, but Mama Kitty would have no part of him. He knew that sooner or later he'd have to catch her and find a safer place for her and her family, but he hoped he'd be able to win her over first. She might be a cat, Lucian thought with a smile, but she was still female, after all. He'd have her purring in his lap in no time.

And speaking of females—Lucian stood in Gabe and Melanie's dining-room doorway and watched the four women busily making decorations for Melanie's baby shower tomorrow. His sister, Cara, with her fourteen-month-old son, Matthew, and his sisters-in-law Abby, Sydney and Melanie were all currently elbow deep in pink and blue tissue paper and string. A pretty sight, he thought, enjoying the sound of their laughter. No reason not to stick around for a while.

And besides, he was certain he smelled cookies.

"Lucian, you're a sweetheart to bring those folding chairs over." Smiling, Abby looked up from the pink tissue flower she was making and tucked a loose strand of blond hair behind her ear. "Callan would have done it but he flew out this morning to meet with the architect on the Thorndale job."

"And Gabe's taken Kevin to the father-son ball game in Pine Flats." Melanie, who'd insisted on helping with the decorations, even though the other women had said no, was making a blue flower. "They won't be home for a couple of hours yet."

"Reese has a waitress on maternity leave and is short-handed." Sydney was busy assembling a centerpiece that said, It's a Baby.

"No sweat." Lucian wandered closer. There were pink and blue balloons, streamers and little baby decorations everywhere. No wonder all the Sinclair men and Cara's husband, Ian, had disappeared. "The Ridgeway project is shut down until Callan gets those changes approved on the blueprints, anyway. I've got all the time in the world right now."

Bingo. Lucian caught sight of a plate of cookies on the table. Unless he missed his mark—and when it came to women and food, he rarely missed—those were Sydney's famous chocolate cookies.

Sydney saw him staring at the plate and held it up. "Cookie?"

"Thought you'd never ask." Lucian moaned as he took a bite of sweet chocolate. "Damn, why did my brother have to marry you first?"

"That's the same line he gave *me* last week when Callan and I had him over for dinner," Abby told Sydney.

"Me, too," Melanie said. "When I baked an apple pie for him three days ago."

"It's the truth, I swear." Lucian held up a hand. "My brothers got the last three women in the entire world that I would have married myself. I'm destined to be alone forever."

All the women rolled their eyes and groaned.

"My entire life I've had to live with this blarney from all four of my brothers." Cara shifted Matthew from one side of her lap to the other. "And from what I hear, dear brother, you aren't exactly wanting for female companionship."

"There've been a lot of devastated women in this town since all my brothers went and got married." Lucian handed a cookie to his nephew, and the baby gurgled with delight. "It's been my duty as the last single Sinclair man to comfort them."

"A job he takes very seriously, from what I'm hearing at the beauty salon." Melanie laid her hands on her rounded belly, then leaned close and whispered, "Sally Lyn Wetters told Annie Edmonds that she was certain Lucian was about to pop the question."

Lucian choked on the cookie he'd just swallowed.

Abby's blue eyes opened wide. "Lucian pop the question to Sally Lyn?"

"She'd make a nice sister-in-law. A little flighty, but sweet," Sydney said. "But Marsha Brenner told me that Laura Greenley and Lucian were an item. Just last week—"

"Hey!" Lucian slammed a fist to his chest and dislodged the stuck cookie. "I'm standing here, you know. And I'm not an item with, or popping any questions to, anybody. Unless, of course—" Lucian grinned at Sydney, Abby and Melanie "—one of you gorgeous ladies decide to dump one of my brothers and run away with me."

"Watch out, ladies, here comes the Sinclair male charm," Abby warned. "There's not a woman alive who can resist it."

"Don't we know it." Sydney arched a brow and smiled. "Not that I'm complaining, you understand."

"Well, there was Raina, Melanie's maid of honor." Cara wiped chocolate from Matthew's cheek. "If I remember correctly, she was quite immune to Lucian's animal magnetism. Melanie had to practically beg Raina to even dance with Lucian at the reception."

Lucian winced at the verbal blow to his pride. "Hey, now, wait just a darned minute. That's not fair. How can I defend myself when I can't even remember that night?"

And not just that night, either. When he'd hit his head in the accident he'd been in the next morning, he'd wiped out nearly two days of his life. He had no memory of even meeting Melanie's friend, let alone dancing with her.

It was the oddest thing, to wake up in the hospital and have absolutely no recollection of the previous forty-eight hours. It was weird and…unsettling. Even now, after all these months, he still couldn't remember anything more than the wedding toast he'd given to Gabe and Melanie that night.

"She was probably playing hard to get." Lucian plucked his nephew from Cara's arms and tossed him up in the air. Matthew shrieked with delight and said, "Mo!" As much as Lucian enjoyed babies, it was especially nice to hand them back over when it was time to go. "I'm sure if she had a little more time to get to know me, I'd dazzle her."

"I'm glad you feel that way." Melanie glanced at her wristwatch. "She's flying in from New York for my baby shower. If you're not too busy, how 'bout you get started dazzling her by picking her up at the airport for me in one hour?"

"Never too busy for you, Mel." He winked at his sister-in-law, then bounced Matthew again, eliciting more giggles. "But I thought you said she was living in Italy."

"She moved her design company to New York two months ago. I'm hoping I can convince her to stay there for good.'' Melanie smiled at the laughing child in Lucian's arms. "You sure you don't mind picking her up?''

"You did say she was single, right?'' Lucian wiggled his eyebrows.

Sydney, Cara and Abby all shook their heads. Chuckling, Melanie wrote her friend's arrival time and flight number on a piece of paper.

"I know you don't remember meeting her, so here's a snapshot from one of the wedding-table cameras.'' Melanie shuffled through a stack of photographs sitting on the table, then handed Lucian the picture. "It should fill in the blank spot in your brain.''

Cara stood and removed her son from Lucian's arms. "You'd need more than a photograph to do that, Mel.''

Lucian raised a brow at his sister's comment, then took the photo from Melanie and looked at it. He'd seen pictures of Raina in Gabe and Melanie's wedding album, but that was over a year ago and it was a group picture. This picture, taken candidly by one of the wedding guests, captured her laughing with Melanie at the reception. Her dress was black and sleeveless and her dark hair was swept up off her long neck. She was more than beautiful.

She was stunning.

A strange feeling, something like a tickle, shimmied up his spine.

"Something wrong?'' Melanie furrowed her brow. "If you'd rather not—''

"Of course nothing's wrong.'' He shook the feeling off, reached for his leather jacket and slipped the picture into his pocket. "I'll have her delivered to you safe and sound and in one piece, m'lady."

"Thank you." Melanie grinned at him. "Oh, and Lucian?"

He'd already started for the door. "Yeah?"

"Would you mind taking my car?"

He lifted a brow. "What, the sophisticated city girl has a problem with trucks?"

Melanie shook her head. "It's just that the baby seat will fit better in the back seat of my car, that's all."

He turned slowly. "Baby seat?"

"Didn't I tell you?" she asked sweetly. "Raina's bringing her baby with her."

It felt good to be on steady ground again, Raina thought with a sigh of relief. The flight, though a short one, had been bumpy, and Emma, normally the sweetest-tempered child, had been unusually cranky. Raina tucked the now-sleeping child in the crook of one arm while she wheeled her carry-on bag with the other. If there was one thing she'd become an expert at after Emma had been born, it was the fine art of juggling. A baby in one hand and a diaper in the other, not to mention a career, time, money and sleep. Sleep being at the bottom of the list.

Hugging Emma close, Raina fell in step with the other passengers pouring off the plane. She'd worked sixteen-hour days this past month to get everything in place for the upcoming show of her new fall line of lingerie. While she was gone, Annelise, her assistant, would handle details, and Raina knew she had nothing to worry about.

But worry or not, Raina wouldn't have missed Melanie's baby shower for anything. After the wedding Melanie had gone on her honeymoon, and Raina had gone to Italy for fourteen months before relocating in New York. There'd been no opportunity to see each other, and between the time difference and the busy lives they both led, they'd only spoken a few, brief times.

But neither time or distance would ever break the bond between them. Melanie was the sister that Raina had never had. They'd grown up together, cried on each other's shoulders in bad times, laughed together in good times. Shared their deepest, darkest secrets.

Most of their secrets, Raina thought, and pressed a gentle kiss to the top of her daughter's soft head.

A man talking on his cell phone in front of her stopped suddenly and she stumbled, gasped when her foot caught on her suitcase. She might have gone down if someone on her left hadn't grabbed her elbow.

She turned with an embarrassed smile. "Thank you. I'm not quite—"

She froze.

Lucian. Lucian Sinclair.

No! her mind screamed. *I'm not ready for this. Not yet.*

Maybe not ever.

He looked at her, those incredible green eyes, and frowned. "Are you all right?"

Of course I'm not all right, damn you! What the hell are you doing here?

"Yes." She croaked the single word out, then cleared her throat. "Yes, of course."

She knew she'd have to see him sooner or later. He was Gabe's brother, after all, and she expected he might drop by the house sometime. She had prepared herself for that. But she'd never expected him here, at the airport. And she *definitely* wasn't prepared.

"Melanie was supposed to pick me up," she said weakly, still struggling to hold on to her composure, though her knees had turned to the consistency of mud, and her mind was still spinning.

"They're holding baby shower tribal council, and she asked me to fill in for her." He kept hold of her elbow while he reached for her suitcase. "Let me get that."

When she kept a death grip on the handle, he looked at her, one brow raised.

I don't want you to get anything for me. Ever, she thought.

"Oh, sorry." She pulled her hand away. "Thank you."

"It's just a suggestion," he said, and nodded at the other deplaning passengers spilling around them, "but we should probably keep moving."

"Right. Of course."

She tried to tug her elbow away from him, but with Emma sleeping in her arms and all the other passengers crowding around her, she had no room to maneuver. So his hand stayed on her, guided her through the river of people.

How well she remembered his hands. Large, callused hands that were strong yet amazingly gentle. Too many nights she'd dreamed of those hands, of his touch. And then she would waken, alone, her body coiled with frustration. With anger. With pain.

She'd remembered every stroke of those long, rough fingers, every breath-stealing kiss of his strong mouth, every sigh and gasp of pleasure. He had touched her where no man ever had before, made her want things she'd never wanted.

And he hadn't even remembered her name.

Lucian, this is Raina...

Raina? Raina who?

Remembering that phone call, the pain and humiliation of it, gave her strength. He'd disrupted her entire world, but she'd meant nothing more to him than a simple roll in the hay. And a forgettable one, at that. She'd be damned if she'd let him see that he'd hurt her. That the night they'd spent together had meant more to her than any other night of her entire life.

So much more, she thought as she hugged her baby closer.

"Do we need to go to baggage claim?" Lucian asked.

She slipped her arm from his hand as she shook her head. "I'm only staying a few days."

"That requires a steamer trunk for most women," he said with a grin.

How could he be so casual with her? Act as if nothing had ever happened?

The smile she gave him was stiff. "Well, I guess I'm not most women."

He raised his brows at her distinctly cool tone. *Dammit, dammit,* she cursed herself. It was one thing to be indifferent and quite another to be rude. If she didn't want him to question her, or to suspect that she felt there had been something more between them than a night of wild sex, then she couldn't very well walk around acting like a shrew.

"I'm sorry." She softened her smile. "It's been a long day, and Emma will be awake soon. If you don't mind, I'd really just like to get back to the house."

Lucian gestured toward the exits. "Your wish is my command."

Yeah, well, then eat dirt and—

The hand he slipped to the small of her back cut off her thought. How dare he put his hand on her so easily? she thought. As if it belonged there? She stiffened inwardly at his touch, pretended that she hadn't even noticed. When he told her that Melanie had put a baby seat in the car for Emma, Raina simply nodded and kept walking.

Thankfully the noise of the crowd inside the airport prevented any normal conversation, and with Emma asleep in her arms, yelling was definitely out of the question. So they walked together, his hand on her, as if they were a couple, which only increased Raina's anxiety level all the more. She didn't want anyone to think that they were together like that. Several women smiled at Emma as they passed. Several *other* women smiled at Lucian.

Why wouldn't they? she thought. He'd certainly blown her socks off when she'd first met him. Six foot four, muscular, broad shoulders and dark good looks. And those eyes of his. Lord, just one glance from those deep-green eyes and a woman could feel her bones melt. It was a handsome package, wrapped with rugged sensuality and tied up with a great big ribbon of pure masculine charm. A present no woman could resist.

She'd known his type well, before they'd met, been married to one. Which was exactly the reason she'd kept her distance at Gabe and Melanie's rehearsal dinner and at the wedding. Instinctively she'd known that this man had the power to hurt her.

Then he'd driven her back to Melanie's house that night. And they were alone. Alone in that great big house, with snow quietly falling outside. He reached for her, or she reached for him. She still wasn't sure. The only thing she was sure of was that once he touched her, once she touched him, there was no going back. She hadn't wanted to go back.

And the next morning he was gone.

"Is something wrong?"

She blinked, realized that they'd walked out of the airport and were standing in the cavern of a parking structure. Lucian held open the back seat door to a black Explorer. She groaned silently, wondered how long she'd been standing there as if she were a complete dimwit.

"No, of course not." She moved toward the open door, then reached inside to settle her still-sleeping daughter into the car seat. She tucked the baby's arms securely inside the shoulder straps, but her fingers were shaking so badly she couldn't manage to snap the metal buckle into place.

"Need some help?" Lucian asked.

Before she could say no, he'd already leaned down beside her and reached inside the car. Her breath caught at the brush of his muscled arm against hers, the touch of his fingers on her own.

Memories flooded back: a long, slow fall to the bed, urgent whispers, bare skin to bare skin. Even the smell of him, a masculine, spicy scent, was the same. Heat rushed up her arms, over her breasts, then spiraled through her body into her blood.

All that in the time it took him to snap the buckle.

Lucian knew he should move away, of course. He'd already clicked the buckle in place, and the baby was snug and secure in the car seat. For some reason he stayed where he was.

In his entire life he couldn't remember when he'd ever been more aware of a woman's presence. The moment he'd first caught sight of her coming off the plane, he'd felt his pulse jump. She'd been easy to spot, not only because every man within twenty feet had also been looking at her, but because she stood a good three inches taller than all the other women around her. And she wasn't even wearing heels. She was long and sleek, her tailored slacks black, her sleeveless turtleneck the color of wine. Her scent was light but exotic. Her dark, shiny hair was pulled back in a thick braid, her bangs a wispy fringe above eyes that made him think of dark-blue smoke.

She might *look* hot, Lucian thought, but good Lord, the woman was cold as an Arctic night. He'd never been attracted to snobs or snooty women before. If anything, the Ice Queen attitude had always been a major turn-off. For some reason, with this woman, it didn't seem to matter. Because here he was, in the most innocent situation, with nothing more than a harmless touch of shoulders and the slightest brush of his leg against hers, and he was aroused.

Down, boy, he reprimanded himself.

There was something about her. Something so incredibly...familiar. Even though he couldn't remember, he knew that he'd met her at the wedding. But this seemed so much more immediate. Much more *intense* than a casual meeting.

But he was certain it hadn't been anything more than that. According to everyone at the wedding, he and Raina had barely spoken. They'd never even been alone.

He'd have to rectify that situation, he decided, but this was hardly the time. Melanie would kill him if he came on to her friend before he even got her back to the house.

But there *was* later, he thought. He didn't know the situation with Raina, didn't know if there was someone in her life, maybe the baby's father or someone else she might be seeing. What he did know was that she was single, and as far as he was concerned, that made her fair game.

Rather than scare the woman off by coming on too strong, Lucian kept his attention on the baby, a dark-haired beauty with rosy cheeks and a turned-up nose. The pink sweater she wore covered a soft, white dress embroidered with pink flowers, and her tiny shoes were pink satin. Everything about her was delicate.

He smiled at the baby. "What's her name?"

"Emma." Raina's voice softened and warmed. She smoothed the front of her baby's sweater. "Emma Rose."

Lucian watched as Raina smoothed the front of Emma's tiny sweater. Her fingers were long and smooth, the stroke of her hand light as a butterfly's wings. He had to remind himself to breathe.

He forced his attention back to the baby. "She's going to break a few hearts."

Raina smiled. "That's what Teresa, Emma's nanny, keeps telling me. She told me to enroll her in a convent now."

The smile on her lips was the first real one he'd seen, Lucian noted. It didn't seem to matter that it wasn't for him. It captivated him all the same.

"If she were my daughter," Lucian teased, "I'm sure I'd feel the same way."

As if he'd flipped a switch, the light in Raina's eyes went dark. The smile was gone, as well.

What had he said?

"She'll be awake soon." Raina pulled away, took a step back from the car. "If she's hungry, the only thing she'll be breaking is your eardrums."

"Well then, we'd better get her home." Lucian had been around long enough to know a brush-off when he heard one. She'd let her guard slip for a moment, but the neon sign that flashed Keep Away was back on.

He quietly closed the back seat door, then opened the front passenger door. If she'd been any other woman, he would have just accepted her blatant rejection. It would certainly be the smart thing to do.

But wasn't she the one who'd told him that she wasn't like most women? And he wasn't always the smartest guy around, either.

With a grin, he closed the car door. If nothing else, Lucian predicted that Raina Sarbanes's visit to Bloomfield was going to make his life extremely interesting.

Two

Gabe and Melanie's house was as beautiful as Raina remembered. Nestled on five acres of pristine farmland, the two-story Victorian had recently been restored to its original beauty by Gabe himself. Outside there was a new coat of paint, Cape Cod blue, with a white porch and trim. Windows sparkled in the late-afternoon light, and daffodils bloomed in the front beds like little bursts of yellow sun. Raina knew that the inside was just as beautiful. High ceilings, shiny hardwood floors, huge fireplaces and a bright, airy kitchen. It was a spectacular house, filled with character and history. And romance, Raina thought with a smile. This house was where Melanie and Gabe had met and fallen in love.

This house, Raina remembered, was also where she and Lucian had made love. In a beautiful, antique, pine-carved four-poster bed, underneath a snowy-white down comforter, between soft-blue flannel sheets—

A bump in the road snapped her back to the moment, and she turned to check on her daughter. Emma had just woken up a couple of minutes ago and was still groggy from her nap. In a few minutes Raina knew that her daughter would be more than ready for a snack and a bottle.

The thirty-minute drive from the airport had been a quiet one. Lucian had been polite, pointing out a landmark here and there and a few more notable points of interest. Raina was relieved, as well as thankful, that he hadn't tried to lure her into anything more than superficial conversation.

Being alone in the car with him and Emma had stretched her nerves thin. The man filled her senses. The sound of his voice, the scent of his skin, the heat of his body. More than once she'd caught herself staring at him. His strong hands on the steering wheel, the square line of his jaw, the slight bend in his nose. Each time, she would jerk her eyes away and curse silently at her weakness.

Thank goodness they were finally here, she thought as he parked the car in front of the house and cut the engine. She'd had a distinct plan before she came to Bloomfield. If she'd had to be alone with Lucian five minutes more, maybe even five seconds more, she was afraid she might have completely blown that plan to smithereens.

She might have come here for Melanie's baby shower, but she had something else to accomplish while she was here. Something more important and more frightening than anything she'd ever faced before.

"Raina!"

Melanie was already out the front door and coming down the porch steps as Raina slid out of the car and rushed toward her. Laughing and with tears in their eyes, the women embraced.

"Oh, look at you, just look at you." Raina swallowed back the tightness in her throat as she touched Melanie's belly. "It's so wonderful."

"And you." Tears were streaming down Melanie's flushed cheeks. "Where is she?"

"Right here." Raina turned back toward the car. "She just woke up, so she may be a little crank—"

Raina went still at the sight of Lucian standing beside the car with Emma high in his arms. She felt as if the breath had been sucked out of her.

"She wanted out," Lucian said as he grinned at the baby. "Since you two were busy, I accommodated her."

Emma smiled back at her rescuer and touched his cheeks. Her hands were so tiny, so white and smooth against Lucian's darker skin.

No! You can't touch her, Raina wanted to scream, but she simply pressed her lips together and bit the inside of her mouth.

"Oh, Rae." Melanie clasped her fingers to her mouth. "Oh, my heavens."

In spite of the situation, Raina couldn't stop the swell of pride and love in her chest. She started to move toward Lucian to take her daughter from him, but Melanie beat her to it.

"Come to your Aunt Melanie." Melanie held out

her hands to the baby. Emma gurgled and smiled but seemed quite content to stay where she was.

"She likes me," Lucian announced, and bounced the baby. Emma giggled with delight.

"She just doesn't know any better." Melanie clapped her hands and coaxed Emma from Lucian's arms.

Now that Melanie was holding Emma, Raina could think clearly again. Slowly she released the breath that had caught in her lungs.

"Isn't she just the most beautiful thing you've ever seen?" Melanie cooed over the baby.

"Absolutely," Lucian said.

Raina glanced at Lucian. Her cheeks warmed as she realized that his gaze was not on Emma but on her. But then her blood warmed from anger. How could he look at her like that? Was he so damn arrogant to think that all he had to do was give her a smoldering I-want-you look and she'd rush right back through that revolving door to his bed and jump in the sack with him?

When he couldn't even remember her name?

She wouldn't respond to his comments or looks, she resolved. She had no regrets for the night they'd spent together, but whatever feelings she'd had for him were gone. Emma was all that mattered to her now. Emma was everything.

The sudden outpour of women from the front porch jarred Raina from her thoughts. Cara, holding her son, Abby and Sydney came rushing forward like a tidal wave. Raina had become close with the women in the two days she'd spent with them all during her last visit, and she looked forward to spending time with them again.

Women.

Lucian shifted awkwardly while they all embraced and gushed over each other, watched as they played musical babies with Matthew and Emma. He might not understand women, but he never tired of looking at them. And these five women were truly something to see. But it was the one he wasn't related to who truly caught his attention.

When she smiled, her face lit up and her eyes sparkled. So maybe ice water didn't run through the woman's veins, after all, he noted. Though she'd been stiff as a two-by-four since he'd picked her up from the airport, she now moved with the grace of a dancer. The sound of her laugh captivated as well as intrigued him. He'd heard that laugh before, he was certain of it. From the video tape of the wedding? Or was he drawing something up from that blank corner of his mind? Occasionally he would almost remember something from the two days he'd lost. A smell, a sound, an image. There'd even been a couple of vague dreams. But nothing had ever been quite this strong before.

Then, just as quickly as it had come on, the feeling was gone, and there was just this moment. Just the sound of a beautiful, though confusing, woman laughing.

Like a Ping-Pong ball, the comments between the women flew back and forth.

"She's got your nose."

"Matthew looks just like his daddy."

"Sydney, you and Reese got married! I'm so happy for you."

"Was Italy wonderful?"

"Abby, I love what you've done with your hair."

And so it went. With five of them, Lucian knew this could go on for quite a while. Sydney held little Emma now, and the baby seemed to be having a conversation of her own with Matthew, who was currently in Abby's arms. The women all laughed and fussed over the two infants. Shaking his head, Lucian turned away and reached into the car to retrieve Raina's luggage and diaper bag.

"You don't have to bother. I'll get that."

He glanced over his shoulder, saw Raina standing behind him. "No bother."

"No, really." She reached for her suitcase as he pulled it out of the car. "I can get it."

For a moment Lucian was distracted by the feel of her hand on his. Her fingers were amazingly soft, her skin smooth. He had the distinct feeling she felt that way all over.

"I'm sure you can." He held on to the suitcase. "But my mother taught me a few lessons in manners. The least I can do is carry a suitcase for a lady."

It was a little heavy-handed, Lucian knew, but it worked. Raina pressed her lips into a thin line, then moved her hand away.

"Thank you," she said, though it was obvious to Lucian it was forced. "But I'll need the diaper bag now."

He handed her the bag, and she hugged it to her. Her eyes met his, and for a moment it seemed as though she wanted to say something.

"I—"

At the sound of Emma's soft cry, Raina quickly glanced over. "It's past time for her snack and bottle," she said awkwardly, then looked back at him. "I...I just want to thank you for picking me up at the airport."

She turned and headed back to her baby. Lucian furrowed his brow as he watched her go. There was something odd about the woman. The way she'd treated him from the moment he'd picked her up at the airport, the way she looked at him, as if there was something on her mind, something she wanted to say. She kept herself composed and in control, but it almost seemed as if under the surface she were angry at him.

He was certain he hadn't done anything to upset the woman in the past hour. Which could only mean that she had to be bothered by something he'd done *before*.

Of course. That had to be it. He must have said something to her at the wedding, or maybe the rehearsal dinner, that had put a bee in her bonnet. But from what everyone had told him, he and Raina had barely spoken to each other.

Jeez, he couldn't very well apologize for something that he couldn't remember. If Raina was ticked off at him, then how difficult could it be to just say so?

He couldn't ask her now, not with everyone around. He'd have to find a moment when they could be alone, which didn't look as if it would be anytime soon. Raina had Emma in her arms, and all the women were heading back to the house, still babbling and fussing over each other. He closed the car door and followed.

"Oh, Lucian." Melanie turned and waited for him on the porch. "Dinner will be ready in a little while and you're staying. Abby made a pot roast, and Sydney made apple dumplings."

"You don't have to ask me twice." He grinned at his sister-in-law. "Where shall I put Raina's bag?"

"In the guest room upstairs." Smiling, she gave him a kiss on the cheek. "Thanks for picking her and Emma up from the airport. She's a very special friend."

"Any friend of yours is a friend of mine," he said, though Raina had been anything but friendly.

And since he was staying for dinner, Lucian thought as he followed Melanie into the house, this would be the perfect opportunity to get the woman alone sometime during the evening and find out why.

"I hit a home run, Mommy. Right off the tee. Daddy helped, but mostly I did it, didn't I, Daddy?"

"You sure did, slugger." Pride lit Gabe's face. "That ball almost went into space."

Kevin's grin widened, and his blue eyes sparkled. "It was way cool, Uncle Lucian. I wish you coulda been there to see me."

"I wish I could have too, pal. Next time for sure." The wink and grin that Lucian gave his nephew made Raina's heart flutter. Lucian had been listening patiently to Kevin since they'd sat down at the dinner table, even though the little boy had been talking nonstop. For a man who'd made it clear he never intended to have children, he certainly was good with them.

All the other women had gone home, leaving just Gabe, Melanie, Kevin, Lucian and herself to eat a huge pot roast and a giant bowl of potatoes and carrots. The food was delicious, but Raina's stomach was so tied up in knots that she had to force herself to eat. Next to her, sitting in a high chair, Emma squealed at Kevin when he stopped talking long enough to chew.

"I think Emma likes you, Kevin," Melanie teased her son.

"Aw, Mom." Kevin groaned like a true six-year-old. "She's a baby."

It was true, though, Raina thought with a smile. Emma had been enthralled with Kevin from the moment he'd walked in the front door. It seemed that all the Sinclair men had that effect on women.

Kevin, on the other hand, wasn't remotely interested in girls or babies. At the moment, baseball was the only thing on Kevin's mind.

And the only thing on Raina's mind was how quickly this meal could be over and how quickly Lucian would leave.

"How 'bout I come by tomorrow?" Lucian said to Kevin. "You can show me exactly how you hit that ball."

"That would be cool." The wide grin on Kevin's face quickly faded. "Oh, yeah, I forgot. I'm not gonna be here 'cause my mom's having a party for our new baby."

"We've been banished for the day." Gabe's sigh

was as exaggerated as it was phony. "From our own home."

"I told you that you could come to the shower if you want to." Melanie cut her son's meat into little pieces, then pointed her fork at Gabe. "You both declined the offer."

"That's 'cause we don't wanna be stuck here with a bunch of girls." Kevin made a face. "You wouldn't want to, would you, Uncle Lucian?"

"I happen to like girls," Lucian said with a grin and glanced at Raina. "Sometimes I like them a lot."

He'd made the comment casually enough, but Raina understood that he'd directed it at her. He was *flirting* with her, in this house, at the dinner table, with Gabe and Melanie watching. Fuming inside, she turned to Emma and offered a bite of potatoes.

The man was a blackheart!

"And they sure like you, too," Kevin said, though his tone was one of disgust. "Every time we go to the grocery store, Cindy Johnson asks my mom about you, and so does that redheaded lady at the post office who laughs real loud. Even Miss Shelly, my teacher at school always says, 'How's your uncle Lucian?' Jeez." Kevin shook his head. "Why don't you just marry one of 'em? Only not my teacher, 'cause I wouldn't wanna call her Aunt Shelly. The other kids would laugh at me."

Raina glanced at Lucian, who at least had the decency to look mildly uncomfortable with Kevin's sudden and excessive information regarding his love life. Not that she was surprised, of course. What else would she have expected from a man like Lucian? He probably threw darts at a board to see who the lucky girl would be for the night.

"As a matter of fact," Melanie said sweetly, "we were just talking about that very thing this morning. Weren't we, Lucian?"

The look Lucian shot Melanie warned her off. "I don't recall."

Amusement danced in Melanie's gray eyes. "Something about comforting all the women of Bloomfield since your brothers got married, I believe. Not wanting to disappoint any of those lonely, single women."

"How magnanimous," Raina said stiffly. When everyone looked at her, she cursed herself for speaking at all.

"We were kidding around." Lucian held out his hands in defense. "Weren't we, Mel?"

Melanie smiled. "So does that mean you *are* going to pop the question to Sally Lyn?"

Raina glanced up sharply at the same time Gabe started to choke. Lucian getting married? Her heart slammed in her chest.

"Sally Lyn?" Gabe hit his chest with his fist. "As in Sally Lyn Wetters? When were you planning to tell me about this?"

"What does pop the question mean?" Kevin asked.

"It means asking someone to marry you," Melanie said.

"Uncle Lucian's getting married?" Kevin's eyes were round with astonishment. "Are you gonna have a big party like my mommy and daddy did?"

"I am *not* getting married," Lucian said fiercely. "And definitely not to Sally Lyn."

"Oh, that's right, I forgot," Kevin went on as if he hadn't heard Lucian at all. "You can't remember my mommy and daddy's party 'cause of your accident. You had a good time, though. You danced with everyone. Even Aunt Raina. So can I come to your party?"

"Kevin," Lucian said with great patience. "I am not getting married and I'm not having—"

"What accident?"

The words were out before Raina could think. The bite of smashed carrots she'd been about to feed Emma hovered in the air. She wasn't sure whether it was the intensity in the tone of her voice or the stunned expression on her face, but everyone, including Kevin, turned to look at her.

"What accident?" she asked again.

"It was no big deal," Lucian protested.

Yes, yes, it is a big deal. Raina's mind raced. *A very big deal.*

"I told you about Lucian's accident the morning after the reception." Melanie furrowed her brow, then said with less certainty, "Didn't I?"

The morning after the reception...

"No." Blood pounded through her veins. "You didn't."

"They knew we'd have cut our honeymoon short if we'd found out he was in the hospital, so they didn't tell us until we got back," Melanie said.

"The hospital?" Raina whispered the two words, turned and stared at Lucian. "You were in the hospital?"

"Just for a couple of days."

Emma started to fuss about the bites coming so

slowly. Raina's fingers shook as she gave her daughter a spoonful of carrot.

"You were in Italy, Rae." Melanie looked apologetic. "And if you remember, we didn't talk for almost three months. I guess by that time, since Lucian was all right, I just didn't think to tell you."

Didn't think to tell me? Oh, dear Lord. Raina swallowed back the scream bubbling up in her throat, struggled to keep her voice calm. She looked at Lucian, held his gaze with her own. "What happened?"

He shook his head. "No idea."

"You mean—" she hesitated "—you don't remember?"

"The police report said that his truck spun out on an icy road sometime around 6:30 a.m." Gabe picked up the glass of merlot he'd been drinking and swirled the red liquid. "Based on the damage to his truck, he's a lucky boy that his injuries weren't worse than they were."

"But you don't remember? Nothing at all?" It was all she could do not to grab him by the shoulders and shake him. "Not even the wedding?"

"Nothing about the wedding, but I did make a toast at the reception that stuck in my head for some reason." Lucian shrugged. "Everyone tells me I had a great time, though, so I guess I'll have to believe them."

Oh, you had a great time, all right, Raina thought. And not just at the wedding. "What's the last thing you *do* remember?" she asked cautiously.

"Driving home after picking up my tux," Lucian said. "That was the day of the rehearsal dinner."

The day she'd come to town, Raina realized. She

and Lucian met for the first time that night, at the rehearsal dinner.

So he didn't remember her. Didn't remember meeting her, dancing with her, driving her back to Gabe and Melanie's…

Making love with her all night.

She suddenly wished she hadn't turned down the glass of wine Gabe had offered her.

"We still haven't figured out the mystery of what he was doing out at that hour of the morning. Especially why he was over at Jordan's Junction." Gabe stared at his glass of wine. "Though we do have a theory."

"Can it, Gabe," Lucian snarled.

"Oh?" Raina white-knuckled the fork in her hand. "And what is it?"

Gabe grinned, obviously enjoying his brother's discomfort. "Well, he still had his tux on, so it's doubtful he even went home. That implies a woman was involved."

"Do you *mind?*" Lucian's eyes narrowed.

"Reese, Callan and Ian had bets down on which one of the constant string of female visitors at the hospital might have been the one, but no one 'fessed up."

"Is that so?" Raina heard the sound of her voice, but it felt disembodied somehow. As if someone else were speaking.

"To this day," Gabe said, as he finished off his wine and set the glass on the table, "she still remains our mystery lady."

Three

It wasn't having too much time on his hands that was driving Lucian crazy. The construction business had always been that way, and he loved that part of his work. Fourteen-hour days for four months on end, then nothing for weeks. Between projects he had the extra hours to spend however he liked, whether it was working on his own house without interruption or jumping on his motorcycle and taking off for days at a time. He had the freedom to stop wherever he wanted, whenever he wanted, for as long as he wanted.

It was a great life. Simple and uncomplicated, with endless choices.

No, having too much time on his hands didn't make him crazy.

Raina Sarbanes was making him crazy. He couldn't

get the woman out of his mind. Even sitting here at the counter in his brother's tavern, with Ian on one side, Callan on the other and a basketball game on the overhead TV, Lucian was thinking about Melanie's best friend.

The woman confused the hell out of him. From the moment he'd picked her up at the airport she'd been cool and blatantly uninterested, then suddenly during dinner she'd shown surprising concern over the accident he'd had after the wedding. Was she just being polite, or had that been genuine concern?

And why would what had happened to him really matter to her at all?

He'd messed up his truck pretty bad, but the accident hadn't been a serious one. He'd had scrapes and bruises, a mild concussion and one hell of a headache for a couple of days, but that was it. Well, except for the fact he'd lost almost two days of his life. But the doctor had told him that memory loss of that nature was not abnormal with the type of head injury he'd sustained. He'd accepted that as no big deal.

But sometimes it *was* a big deal, he thought. Sometimes he had the strangest feeling that it was a *very* big deal.

He'd tried to get Raina alone last night after dinner to ask her if he'd offended her in some way at the wedding, but she'd conveniently disappeared upstairs with her baby and hadn't come back down. Today was the shower, so he couldn't go over there now, either.

Lucian frowned as he picked up the mug of beer he'd been nursing for the past half hour. Patience had never been his strong suit.

Cheers erupted all around him when Allen Iverson with the 76ers shot a buzzer beater to upset the favored New York Knicks. Callan and Ian both slapped Lucian on the back at the same time and beer sloshed out of his mug.

"Hey, careful when a man's got a beer in his hand," Lucian complained.

"And a woman on his mind." Reese stepped up from the other side of the bar and wiped up the spill.

"Who's the lucky lady today?" Callan handed Ian the five bucks he'd just lost on the game.

"What makes you think I've got a woman on my mind?" Lucian scowled at his brothers and brother-in-law. "There are other things that occupy my time and attention when I'm not working, you know."

The other three men looked at each other, then back at him.

"Was he watching the game?" Ian asked Callan.

"Nope."

"Was he working on his house today?" Ian asked Reese.

Reese shook his head. "Not that I know of."

"Has he even been drinking that beer Reese gave him a half hour ago?"

They looked at the full mug of beer, then at each other. "It's a woman," Ian, Callan and Reese said together.

"Come on, bro, out with it." Reese pulled the warm beer out of Lucian's hand and dumped it, then filled a fresh mug. "So what's up?"

"Nothing's up." Just to prove it, he took a long pull on the ice-cold amber brew.

Ian snagged a peanut from a bowl on the counter

and cracked it open. "Cara said you were tripping over your tongue when you brought Melanie's friend back from the airport. What's her name, Rita?"

"So I looked, so what?" He shrugged. "I'm not blind or dead, you know. And her name's *Raina*," he added, "not Rita."

"Raina, that's right."

Ian grinned at him, and Lucian knew he'd been had.

"Look, sorry to disappoint you girls." Lucian gave the other men a bored look and took another sip of his beer. "But it's just not there."

"It's not there on her part, anyway." Callan wasn't about to miss an opportunity to let a dig pass by. "Obviously, the woman is as smart as she is gorgeous."

Lucian gritted his teeth. Maybe, just maybe, he thought, if he ignored them they'd all go away. And if he believed that, he might as well go out and buy some beach property next to Sam Peterson's dairy farm.

If anything, Lucian knew from experience that they were just getting started.

"Uncle Ian! Uncle Callan! Uncle Reese! I hit a home run yesterday." Kevin came bounding up to the bar with Gabe close behind. The boy swung his arms in a reenactment. "You know, Uncle Lucian."

"Right outta the park, pal." Talk about timing, Lucian thought with a thankful smile. There was nothing like a loquacious six-year-old to curb a discussion about women. "I taught the boy everything he knows."

"I'd say that calls for a celebration." Reese caught

the eye of a petite redheaded waitress. "Marie, a burger and chocolate shake here for my nephew."

"Wow! Thanks Uncle Reese." Kevin climbed up on the bar stool. "And we should celebrate Uncle Lucian, too, since he's getting married."

Lucian nearly spit out the beer he'd just sipped. Except for the wail of a Willie Nelson song about being on the road—which was exactly where he'd like to be right now—it seemed as though the entire restaurant had gone quiet. Every head in the place turned and looked at him. Ian, Reese and Callan, brows raised, all stared.

Gabe, on the other hand, grinned and slipped onto the stool beside his son.

So much for curbing the conversation, Lucian thought with a sigh. With his luck, the headline of the *Bloomfield County Gazette* would be his impending marriage.

"I am *not* getting married," he said firmly and with as much patience as he could muster under the circumstances. "Not to anyone. You all got that?"

All the men gave each other a knowing look, then turned their attention back to Kevin, who'd thankfully changed the conversation back to baseball.

Lucian took another sip of beer and shook his head. For crying out loud, what was with all this marriage talk lately?

Married people just couldn't stand seeing single people happy, that was it. Couldn't believe that they were truly happy. Which he was. He *liked* being single and intended to stay that way for a very, very long time. Maybe forever.

It would take a very special woman to change his

mind, Lucian thought, and in his heart he truly didn't believe that woman existed.

"Oh, Rae, just look at this." Melanie's eyes shone brightly with tears as she clutched the tiny, white, knit hat in her hands. "Isn't this just the most precious thing you've ever seen?"

"It's lovely." Smiling, Raina set Emma down beside a pile of empty gift boxes, and the baby shrieked with delight. "See, Emma likes it, too."

"She was an angel today." Melanie offered the baby a bright red-and-blue rattle that had been on top of one of the packages. "Is she always that good around so many people?"

Raina sat down on the sofa beside Melanie, thankful for the quiet. The decibel level of thirty women at a baby shower was equal to that of a jet plane landing in a thunderstorm. The last person, including Melanie's sisters-in-law, had left just a few minutes ago, but Raina's ears were still ringing.

"She was practically born in a dressing room filled with models. She was adored by so many different women, I was afraid she wouldn't even know who her real mother was. I had to hire a nanny just so the child could have a little peace." Raina picked up a pale-green sleeper and felt a tug in her heart. "I can't even remember when she was this small."

"Rae." Melanie's smile faded as she took Raina's hand. "I'm so sorry I couldn't be there for you when you were pregnant with Emma. You know how much I wanted to be."

"Of course I know that." Raina gave her friend a hug. "I was in Italy, working sixteen-hour days. You were here, with Kevin and a brand-new husband. We were both where we belonged at that time, doing what we needed to be doing.''

Melanie nodded sadly, then leaned back and looked at Raina thoughtfully. ''Why haven't we ever talked about it?''

Raina glanced away, watched Emma toss the rattle into an empty box and chortle with laughter. *We never talked because I'm a coward,* Raina wanted to say but couldn't.

Because I was terrified you'd ask who Emma's father was.

She hadn't even told Melanie that she was pregnant until she was six months along. Raina knew that had hurt Melanie, but she also knew that Melanie would understand, that she would forgive her and be patient. Melanie had always been all the things that Raina had not.

''I'm sorry,'' Raina said quietly. ''I wasn't trying to shut you out. I didn't want you to worry about me, and I...I was confused. There were some things I wasn't ready to face.''

''Are you ready now?''

Melanie's quiet question resonated through Raina. She glanced at her daughter, felt that same overwhelming wave of love wash over her.

Was she ready?

Her mind was still reeling from the bombshell that had been dropped on her last night at the dinner table: Lucian had been in an accident the morning after the wedding.

After she'd changed the bedding and straightened up any traces of Lucian having spent the night there,

Raina had packed her bags and called for a taxi to take her to the airport. She'd boarded her plane and left the country, all the time thinking that he'd walked out on her without even a thank-you-ma'am.

And three months later, when she'd made the most difficult phone call of her life…

Lucian, this is Raina…

Raina? Raina who?

The confusion in his voice, then the long silence that had followed had been like a knife in her heart. It was one thing to think he'd walked away from her without so much as a backward glance, but that he couldn't even remember her name was more than she could bear. Without another word she'd hung up the phone and never called back.

An *accident*. He'd left her and been in an accident.

She'd lain awake most of last night, tossing and turning in that same bed that she and Lucian had made love in. Images kept flashing in her mind: Lucian's truck spinning off an icy road. Lucian lying hurt and bleeding, alone in a ditch. Lucian lying in a hospital bed, his head bandaged and his body bruised.

He'd said at the dinner table that it was no big deal, but he had no idea how wrong he was. It *was* a big deal.

A very big deal.

She realized, of course, that she still had no idea what his intentions were when he'd left her that morning. If he'd come back, or if he'd called her. She would never know that now.

Because *he* didn't even know.

He couldn't remember. He didn't remember the night they'd spent together, didn't remember very much of the wedding, didn't even seem to remember meeting her, from what little she could gather.

She closed her eyes, struggled to breathe against the weight on her chest. All the hurt and anger she'd felt since that night turned to guilt. Somehow she had to make things right.

If only she knew how.

"Rae."

The sound of Melanie's soft voice snapped Raina out of her musings. Was she ready? Melanie had asked.

No. She wasn't ready. But she had no choice.

"There's something I have to do." Raina squeezed Melanie's hand. "Then I'll tell you everything before I leave here. I promise."

"I'll hold you to that," Melanie said, squeezing Raina's hand right back. "Now before Tornado Kevin and Gabe come blasting through the door, why don't we—" she stopped, listened "—too late. Hold on to your seat."

The front door flew open, and Kevin exploded into the room. Raina's heart skipped when hot on his heels came Lucian. Like two banshees, they ran through the living room into the kitchen.

Wide-eyed, Emma stared.

Gabe strolled in through the open door and closed it behind him. Smiling, he headed for his wife and bent down to give her a kiss.

"Let me guess," Melanie said. "They heard there was cake here."

"Yep. Word has it that it's chocolate with whipped cream."

"With raspberry filling," she added. "I hid a piece for you in the fridge."

"That's my girl." He kissed her again, then scooped Emma up off the floor. "And speaking of girls, how's my favorite little one?"

"Ready for a bath and bedtime," Raina answered. Now that Lucian had showed up, Raina was anxious to go upstairs. She knew they needed to speak, and soon, but this was hardly the time. "Come on, sweetie, let's give Uncle Gabe and Aunt Melanie a little alone time."

"Can we put her to bed?" Melanie asked, and grinned at her husband. "I'm out of practice, and Gabe could use a few lessons."

"You mean they don't come with an instruction book?" he asked, tickling Emma's belly. The baby giggled and grasped at Gabe's hand for more.

"Sure they do." It required a helping hand from Gabe, but Melanie managed to push herself out of the sofa. "And all the pages are blank. Same as that book titled, *What Men Know about Women.*"

A loud thud came from the kitchen, a whoop of laughter, then Kevin came out a moment later, wiping chocolate crumbs from his face with the back of his hand. Melanie frowned at her son.

"I beat Uncle Lucian in an arm wrestle for the first piece of cake," Kevin announced proudly.

"Upstairs, young man," Melanie said firmly. "In the tub, then pj's on."

"Aw, Mom." Kevin headed for the stairs. "I'm not tired at all."

"Last time you said that you fell asleep on top of

your bed," Gabe said. "In your underwear, if I re-call."

"Did not!" Kevin's face turned bright red as he looked from Raina to his father. "I was just resting."

He scampered up the stairs ahead of his parents, with Emma chattering at him. When Raina started to rise from the sofa, Melanie waved her back. "You just stay right here."

"But—"

"No buts," Melanie said as she slowly made her way up the stairs. "We'll be down as soon as Emma's asleep. You just relax until we get back."

Relax? Raina would have laughed if her throat wasn't so tight with nerves. With Lucian in the kitchen and everyone else upstairs, relaxation was the furthest thing from her mind.

"Hey."

She drew in a slow breath, then glanced over her shoulder at the sound of his voice behind her. Why did the man always have to look so damn appealing? she thought irritably. In her line of work she was constantly surrounded by men dressed in tailored, fashionable clothes, and all this man had to put on to look incredibly sexy was a pair of faded jeans and a snug black T-shirt.

She swallowed down the tightness in her throat and forced a smile. "Hello."

He held a paper plate with a hefty slice of cake in one hand and a fork in the other. He sauntered toward her, kept those incredible green eyes on her as he sat down on the sofa beside her.

"Looks like Melanie got a nice load of loot here." He gestured toward all the open presents lying around them, then pointed at a box sitting on the coffee table. "What's that thing?"

"A baby monitor." She busied herself by folding a white baby blanket, prayed that he wouldn't notice her hands were shaking. "It has dual receivers."

"No kidding? What will they think of next?" He grinned at her, took a bite of cake and groaned. "Damn, this is good."

It was making her crazy. Lucian sitting so close to her, grinning that Sinclair grin that made women weak. Even the way he ate that cake was sexy, she thought, all that chocolate and whipped cream he'd scooped into that handsome mouth of his, the way his eyes glinted with pleasure.

She remembered a night he'd looked at her that way, as if he'd wanted to gobble her up whole. She shivered at the memory.

"Cold?"

"Not at all," she said quickly, and reached for another baby blanket.

He nodded at a wicker bassinet sitting on the floor. "Don't tell me they're going to put my nephew in that oversize bread basket."

"What makes you think it's a boy?" Gabe and Melanie had chosen not to be told the baby's sex, but that didn't stop the family from speculating. "It could just as easily be a girl, you know."

"Could be, but I've got ten bucks down it's a boy." He looked at her thoughtfully. "Did you find out Emma was a girl before she was born?"

Raina felt her pulse quicken. This was definitely not an area of conversation she wanted to explore.

Not yet, anyway. She leaned forward to straighten the boxes Emma had been playing with on the floor.

"I knew."

"So you didn't want to be surprised?"

"No." She glanced up at the sound of water splashing from the bathtub upstairs, heard Emma's screech of pleasure, then Melanie and Gabe's laughter. "I think I should go—"

"Raina." He set his cake down on the coffee table, then reached out. "Wait."

The last thread of composure slipped when she felt his hand circle her wrist. She sat back down, but only because her knees wouldn't have supported her, anyway.

"What?" she said, and cursed the fact her voice sounded more like one of Cinderella's mice.

"Why do I make you so nervous?"

"I'm not nervous." *Big lie.* They both knew it.

"I've been thinking about you." His thumb brushed lightly back and forth over her wrist. "Wondering why you act so differently around me than anyone else. Was it something I did? Something I said at the wedding or before?"

"No." That at least was true. "It was nothing you said."

"Your pulse is racing," he murmured. "So it was something I did, then. Tell me. Please."

The soothing tone of his voice, the velvet touch of his thumb on her skin mesmerized her. "It…it wasn't at the wedding or before."

"So when was it?"

She closed her eyes, swallowed hard. "It was after."

Four

"After?" Based on the somber look on Raina's face and the serious look in her eyes, Lucian decided whatever he'd done, it must have been pretty bad. "Someone said you went back to Gabe and Melanie's house after the reception. I assumed that Cara and Ian took you back."

"They were going to," Raina said quietly. "But Cara was six months pregnant, and I could see she was exhausted. I told them to go ahead and I'd find a ride with someone else."

The implication hovered between them for a moment, then Lucian raised both brows. "Are you saying that *I* took you?"

"You were taking the wedding gifts over to Gabe and Melanie's, anyway. It made sense I would just ride along with you."

"But why didn't anyone know we left together?" he asked. "Someone must have seen us."

"You were loading your truck through the back door of the reception hall and we drove out from the back parking lot. Maybe in all the confusion of everyone leaving at once, they thought you'd left before me, instead of with me."

He hated this, having a blank spot in his brain. It had driven him nuts at first, but he'd simply accepted that other than the wedding toast he'd made to Gabe and Melanie, he would probably never remember anything about that night or the day before.

He felt the rapid-fire beat of her pulse under his fingertips, the icy chill of her skin. Like a punch in his gut, he realized what she was trying to tell him.

Oh, hell...

"Are you saying that I...that we..."

She nodded. "We spent the night together."

Oh, hell.

"Raina, my God, I...I don't know what to say." He'd been in a situation or two, but nothing that ever came close to this. "I didn't, I mean, was I—"

Damn. He didn't know *what* to say.

They'd *slept* together. Spent the night together— here in this house.

"And you never said anything?" he finally managed. "Not even to Melanie?"

"There was no reason to tell Melanie. What happened was between you and me."

"But you never said anything to me, either." He struggled to find some kind of balance. "Why?"

"I was asleep when you left the next morning." She pulled her hand from his, tucked it under her leg.

"There was no note when I woke up and you didn't come back so I thought—"

"That I was a complete jerk. Jeez." Her hostility toward him at the airport made all the sense in the world. Good Lord, he was lucky she hadn't decked him one. "Look, Raina, I have no idea where I went, but I swear to you I wouldn't have just taken off like that without saying goodbye."

"I didn't know about your accident." She leaned toward him. "If I had, I never would have just left like I did, either."

He tried to absorb the impact of what she'd just told him, but it felt as if he'd been dealt a knockout blow and couldn't quite grab the ropes to pull himself up.

They'd made love. He still couldn't believe it.

And dammit to hell, he couldn't remember.

"Lucian." She glanced up at the muffled sound of Melanie singing "Rock-a-Bye Baby" to Emma, then looked back at him. "In spite of how this may sound to you, and the fact that we'd only just met, it wasn't casual sex. Impulsive, yes, unexpected, absolutely. But it wasn't casual."

"Damn." Shaking his head, he dragged a hand through his hair. "Of all the things I would never want to forget, it would be making love with you."

She blushed at his words. "Lucian—"

"So you're the mystery woman." He reached for the hand she'd tucked under her leg, glanced down as he traced the ridge of her knuckles with his thumb. "According to my family you were less than enamored with me. How did it…I mean, how did we—"

He paused. Damn, but this was awkward. He was

on unfamiliar territory here, not knowing what had happened or how, certainly not knowing what to say. How was he supposed to ask for details without sounding crude?

At the sound of a door closing upstairs, Raina quickly pulled her hand from his. "We need to talk, Lucian, but this isn't the right time."

He nodded. This was definitely not the right time. He heard Melanie and Gabe talking to Kevin in the hallway upstairs, and Lucian knew he'd better leave now, before they came back down. He was still dazed from what Raina had told him, and Gabe would know something was up.

"I'll be over in the morning. I promised Kevin we'd hit some balls out back."

He held her gaze as he stood and pulled her up with him. Unable to stop himself, he touched her cheek with his fingertip, noticed her sharp intake of breath and soft flutter of her lashes as she glanced down. Oh, yeah, he thought. There was something here, and it wasn't just on his side, either.

"Tomorrow," he whispered.

"Yes," she answered. "Tomorrow."

He left then, wondering how that single word could hold such promise and apprehension at the same time.

"Lucian is not going to like this one little bit." Shaking her head, Melanie pulled fresh, warm bagels out of a brown paper bag and set them in a basket on the kitchen table. "He hates surprises."

"That's what makes it so much fun," Cara said as she added sliced bananas to a bowl of mixed fruit. "He won't even know what hit him until he walks through that door. Ian," she called into the living room where the other men had gathered. "You have film in the camera?"

"All set," Ian called back to his wife.

Purple and red birthday balloons had replaced pink and blue baby shower decorations and a banner printed from Abby's computer read, Happy Birthday, Lucian. Sydney stood at the kitchen counter drizzling icing on the cinnamon rolls she'd baked, and Abby was at the stove frying bacon. The house was filled with all the wonderful scents and sounds of a family Sunday brunch.

If there was one thing that the Sinclair clan enjoyed, Raina noted as she watched all the hustle and bustle, it was a party. It didn't seem to matter that just yesterday they'd had a baby shower for Melanie. A birthday was a birthday, after all, and whether Lucian wanted it or not, his family intended to celebrate.

Not a moment had passed since he'd left last night that she hadn't thought about him. While her daughter had slept soundly in the bedroom next to her own, Raina had spent most of her night tossing and turning, listening to the soft hum of the new baby monitor Melanie had set up. The sound had been a soothing comfort to her while she struggled to find the right words to tell Lucian about Emma.

Tomorrow, she'd said to him.

And tomorrow was now today.

His birthday, no less. She hadn't known about that until last night when Melanie mentioned the surprise brunch they were giving him this morning. If she had known, she never would have promised to talk with him today.

Of all the days to tell a man he had a seven-month-old child.

Nerves clawed at her stomach, and she felt as if a fist had hold of her chest. She knew there was no way he would let her put it off. He wanted to know the truth about what had happened that night. She understood that; he had a right.

If only she'd known about the accident, that he'd been in the hospital and lost the memory of those precious hours they'd spent together the night before. Everything might have been so different....

But she hadn't known, and life was full of if-onlys. She could only deal with the here and now.

"Raina, will you please fill this and set it on the dining room table?" Melanie pulled a container of orange juice out of the refrigerator and set it next to a glass pitcher on the table. "He's going to be here any minute and I still need to get the coffee going."

Eager for any little job to occupy her mind and hands, Raina opened the carton, then filled the pitcher and went into the dining room. In the living room Reese was on guard for Lucian. Callan was holding Emma, and Gabe held Matthew. To both babies' delight, Kevin was jumping up and down and making faces.

She couldn't help but smile, felt her eyes tear up at the sound of her daughter's laughter.

"They do that to you," Cara said from behind her. "Make you weepy and emotional over the smallest things. I bawled like a baby myself the first time Matthew smiled at me."

Coffee creamer in hand, Melanie joined Cara and Raina. "I couldn't even speak when they handed

Kevin to me in the hospital.'' Melanie touched her stomach, then blinked furiously. ''Oh, dear, here I go again with the waterworks. Gabe's nickname for me these days is Niagara.''

Raina and Cara both smiled with understanding and wiped at their own tears as they all hugged. Melanie was the only family Raina had ever known. In spite of everything, it felt good to be back.

''He's here!''

Raina's pulse jumped at Reese's announcement. Laughing and whispering, everyone scrambled to gather in the living room. Raina took Emma from Callan and stood back.

Lucian opened the door.

''Surprise!''

He stood in the doorway, startled for a moment, then shook his head with a groan and looked heavenward. Ian snapped a picture.

''Lord save me from this crazy family,'' he said, but there was no bite to his words. Grinning, he hugged and kissed Cara and his sisters-in-law in turn, and endured the digs and back slapping from all the men.

Nervous and a little overwhelmed, Raina held back, smiling at the festivities, but not comfortable enough to jump into the middle of it all. When Lucian moved toward her with a grin on his face, panic gripped her.

Before she could recover, he had his arms around her and had pulled both her and Emma close.

The warmth of his body against her own, the masculine scent of his skin, the rock-solid feel of his arms around her, everything went straight to her head. It was impossible to breathe, to think, even to react. She heard the sound of voices around her, saw the flash of Ian's camera, but her entire focus was on Lucian.

When he lightly brushed his lips across her cheek, lingered there for just a moment, her heart slammed in her chest.

Emma touched his cheek and gurgled, and the camera flashed again.

"So you were in on this conspiracy, were you?" He pulled away from her, then poked a finger in Emma's soft belly. "Did you know your mommy was so sneaky?"

Still not fully recovered from the unexpected contact with Lucian, Raina simply smiled, did her best to look composed, when in reality she was shaking inside.

"Food's on."

Carrying a steaming metal pan of ham-and-cheese quiche, Sydney came into the dining room through the swinging kitchen door. All the men teased Lucian, who took the ribbing good-naturedly. Since he was the birthday boy, Lucian sat at the head of the table and the women filled his plate for him, but the rest of the men were on their own.

They were an exuberant bunch, Raina thought as she watched food exchange hands and jokes fly. When she'd come in for the wedding, there'd been no time for relaxed family get-togethers. The rehearsal dinner at Reese's tavern had been hectic, followed by the wedding and reception the next day. The two days had flown by.

And after the reception, Raina thought, that part of the night had passed *much* too quickly.

As if he'd read her thoughts, Lucian glanced up at

her, held her gaze while he nodded at Callan, who was discussing the architectural changes on an upcoming project their company was scheduled to build. She should have looked away, told herself to, but she couldn't. She stared back, mesmerized, as if they were the only two people in the room....

Raina blinked, realized that Abby, who was sitting beside her had asked her a question. "Excuse me?"

"Melanie mentioned that you have a show coming up in a few weeks," Abby repeated.

"Two weeks." Raina forced herself not to think about Lucian, or that the conversation had now turned to her. "It's a new fall line of lingerie."

All the mens' heads snapped to attention. Melanie frowned and pointed a finger at her husband. "Say one word, Gabe Sinclair, and you're sleeping on the sofa tonight."

"What?" Gabe's expression was one of complete innocence. "I was just going to ask for some watermelon."

Groans and laughter circled the table, and though she tried to look angry, Melanie just shook her head with exasperation. Raina watched the two of them, saw the special look they exchanged and couldn't remember when she'd ever seen two people more in love.

She realized that every couple sitting here seemed to have that special look for each other, that look that was only for their mate, a look of love and respect that no words could express.

She'd been married for one year when she was twenty-two. Nicholas Sarbanes. He'd been handsome, wealthy, charming. Too late she'd realized that Nicholas had only wanted a trophy wife, a woman to look good on his arm and impress everyone in his exclusive circle of wealthy friends. She'd been dazzled for a few weeks by all the glitz and glamour and attention, but it had worn off quickly after they were married, as had his so-called love for her. She'd only been one in a long string of models he couldn't seem to keep his hands off.

Nicholas had never once looked at her the way these men were looking at their wives. No man ever had. They had looked at her with lust or desire, but not with the kind of love surrounding her at the moment. A love that endured. A love that was as endless as it was timeless. Love that spoke volumes in one word or no word at all. Love that was a look only two people understood.

"What's lawngeray?" Kevin asked while pulling a cinnamon roll apart.

"It's underwear for women," Melanie answered.

"Oh." Kevin turned the same color as the watermelon in the fruit bowl. "Why would anyone wanna see a show for *that?*"

Everyone chuckled, but no one seemed to want to answer the six-year-old's question, so the conversation moved swiftly on to basketball play-offs and one-year checkups for babies.

"The Lakers will never do it this year. Not with two key players out with injuries."

"All those shots were a nightmare. I cried as hard as Matthew."

"The Knicks are a shoe-in this year. Their center is hot."

"We've got five more months before Emma's appointment. I'm already dreading it."

Lucian teeter-tottered between listening to discussions about basketball shots and babies' shots. If Raina hadn't been at the table, he would have concentrated completely on basketball, but he found himself wanting to know more about the woman.

He'd passed on a poker game with Reese and the McDougall brothers last night. Instead he spent his evening pacing and thinking about Raina. Lord knew he had a lot to think about.

He still couldn't believe that they'd made love. Well, he believed it. He had no doubt that Raina was telling the truth. Why would she lie about something like that? He just couldn't *believe* it.

Just his luck. He'd made love to the most beautiful woman he'd ever seen in his life and he couldn't remember one damn minute of it. God had one hell of a sense of humor.

She must have thought him a complete idiot when he never came back or even said goodbye to her. In spite of the rumors regarding his love life, he'd never been promiscuous and he'd never been cruel. That wasn't his style.

He had so many questions—questions that she'd promised to answer today. He was chomping at the bit to get her alone, but now that his family had planned a birthday party for him, he knew he would have to wait. It was making him nuts.

While Gabe and Callan argued over who'd sunk the most baskets so far this season, Lucian turned his attention from Raina to little Emma. She was every bit as beautiful as her mother, though now that he thought about it, the child didn't really have Raina's features. Other than Emma's dark curls, the child looked more like she would belong to his sister. Especially those big green eyes, Lucian thought. They were exactly the same shade as Cara's.

And Gabe's. And Reese's.

And...*his*.

He frowned, felt his heart skip a beat. Emma's hair wasn't the same shade as Raina's, either.

It was darker...like his.

Lucian looked at Matthew and Emma, sitting next to each other, both of them in high chairs. They were so close in age, they almost looked like twins.

Or cousins.

His heart started to pound a little faster. No. It wasn't possible. Emma was seven months old, the wedding was—he stopped, did the math.

Oh, God.

He stood suddenly, kept his narrowed gaze on Raina. She'd been talking, but stopped in the middle of a sentence as she watched him walk around the table toward her. Her eyes widened with confusion, then fear.

He took her by the arm, felt a tic jump in his temple as he said, "We need to talk."

"Lucian!" Melanie stared at him in shock. Frowning, Gabe started to stand.

"Gabe, you stay out of this," Lucian said tightly. "I'm sorry, Melanie, but you'll all have to excuse Raina and me."

Melanie opened her mouth to protest, but Raina shook her head. "It's all right, Mel."

Melanie pressed her lips into a thin line and leaned back in her chair. Everyone else just stared.

His hand circling her arm, he practically dragged her up the stairs into the first bedroom, which happened to be the nursery.

He closed the door behind them and ignored Raina's gasp of shock when he brought her up against him.

"Tell me," he said in a low growl. "Is Emma my child?"

Five

Raina felt the blood drain from her head. What had happened? One minute they'd all been sitting around the table laughing and talking, the next minute he'd come at her with an intensity in his eyes that had, quite literally, taken her breath away. She hadn't had time to prepare or think or react.

She blinked at him, unable to speak, then gasped when he tightened his hold on her arm.

"Is she?" he asked again.

She yanked away from him, rubbed her arm as she stepped back. Whatever the situation, she refused to be manhandled. "This is hardly the time to have this discussion."

"She is, isn't she?" He stared at her, disbelief etched sharply in the tight lines on his face. "When you told me last night that we slept together after the wedding, I should have realized immediately. It doesn't take a rocket scientist to add up the months and figure it out.''

"Lucian, I—"

"She's got my eyes, my hair." He dragged a hand through that hair as he shook his head. "She's got Sinclair written all over her, and I didn't even see it until this minute. Dammit, Raina, why the *hell* didn't you tell me?"

"When?" She felt her own anger rise. "The next morning when I woke up and you were gone without a word? Oh, well, since I hardly knew I was pregnant then, I guess not."

"You could have—"

"What? Called you when I found out?" She narrowed her eyes. "For your information, I did call you. You didn't even know who I was. 'Raina who?' you said. Have you any idea how that felt?"

"For God's sake." He threw his hands out in frustration. "I didn't remember because I *couldn't* remember."

"Will you please lower your voice?" she hissed, then sucked in a breath. "Lucian, I'm not clairvoyant. Since Melanie and I had never talked about it, I had no way of knowing about your accident. All I knew was that I was in Italy, unmarried, pregnant and the father of my baby couldn't even remember my name. I did what I had to do."

A muscle worked in his jaw as he started to pace. "Why didn't you at least tell Melanie about this?"

"As far as I knew, you couldn't even remember my name." Raina shook her head. "Do you really think I would call my best friend and put her in the middle of a situation like that? Tell her that I had a wild night of sex with her brother-in-law, who had made it clear he wanted no commitments in his life? For the first time in her life, Melanie was—is—happy. She certainly doesn't need me putting any strain or stress on that happiness.''

Lips pressed in a hard line, he stopped his pacing and moved toward her. ''I had a right to know that I had a child.''

Raina closed her eyes and nodded. ''After that phone call, and even right after Emma was born, I admit that I wasn't going to tell you, but then—'' she paused, wanting to choose her words carefully ''—then I realized that you *needed* to know. I have no family. If anything ever happened to me, Emma would be alone. That thought terrified me.''

''You were going to tell me because you thought I *needed* to know, not because you thought I would *want* to know?''

''That night we both made it clear that we weren't looking for love or permanence or commitment in a relationship,'' she said carefully. ''No marriage plans, no children. Why would I think you'd changed your mind?''

The night might have started that way, she remembered, though it hadn't ended that way. At least, not for her. By the end of that night, she hadn't wanted it to end. She'd already fallen in love with him.

And then he was gone.

''Lucian.'' She said his name on a sigh. ''I had no idea what you wanted, but from the moment I learned I was pregnant, I wanted that baby more than anything I've ever wanted in my life. Emma is my world."

Eyes narrowed, jaw tight, he stared at her but said nothing. The tension stretched, but still he said nothing.

The distant sound of Emma's cry from downstairs brought them both back to reality.

He stepped away, still staring at her with those cool green eyes, then turned and left the room.

Raina released the breath she'd been holding, waited a moment and followed. Her heart sank as she heard Lucian's truck start up then drive away.

At the insistent sound of Emma's cry, Raina had no choice but to go to her daughter and face Lucian's family.

She sucked in a breath, lifted her chin and walked downstairs. Everyone but Kevin and Gabe were still sitting in the dining room, and they all looked at her as she walked in.

"I...I'm sorry," she started to explain, though she had no idea what she was going to say. "Lucian and I, we..."

"Raina, you don't have to say anything." Melanie stood with a tired, fussy Emma in her arms. "I'm sorry. I turned it off, but not before, I mean, not before—"

Confused, Raina glanced in the direction that Melanie's gaze had drifted, to an oak sideboard in the dining room.

Oh, God.

Raina's heart stopped as she stared.

The baby monitor.

Dread raced through her as she looked back at

everyone. She had no idea exactly how much they'd heard, but it was clear they'd heard enough.

Oh, God.

"Now *that*—" Reese was the first to break the awkward, horrible silence "—is what I call a surprise party."

Lucian pulled a nail from the pouch at his waist, positioned it at the corner of the two-by-four and swung the hammer. The nail slammed into the wood in one smooth hit. He swore, set the next nail, swung the hammer again. And swore.

Another nail, another swing, another curse.

He'd been at it for nearly two hours. Hammering, swearing. Thinking.

I'm a father.

I have a daughter.

Emma is my baby.

Father. Daughter. Baby.

It had taken two hours, plus several dozen nails and four smashed knuckles for the reality to sink in: he was a father. Emma's father.

That was one hell of a birthday present.

With a heavy sigh he dropped the hammer into his work belt, then scrubbed a hand over his face. He'd barely had time to accept the bombshell that he and Raina had spent the night together before the second bomb had hit. He had a kid. He'd been a father for seven months and he hadn't even known.

"Dammit." He kicked a sawed-off block of wood off the porch and sent it sailing into the nearby woods. She should have told him. He'd had a right to know.

He'd gone over it in his mind, again and again, struggled to make sense of it, to understand. But it was damn hard when he couldn't remember a blasted thing about the night they'd spent together.

He tried to put himself in her place, picture everything that had happened from her point of view: they make love; she thinks he's ducked out on her; she finds out she's pregnant; she calls him; he doesn't remember her name; she decides to raise the baby herself and not tell him because she thinks that he wouldn't want a child.

But no matter how hard he tried, no matter how many times he went over the scenario, it came back to the same thing: Emma was *his* baby, too.

Raina might have thought him a louse, but to keep his own child from him—he felt a fresh wave of anger roll through him and kicked another block of wood.

No matter what the circumstances, that was unforgivable.

Dammit! If only he could remember even just one little thing about that night.

She said that they had talked, that he'd told her he wasn't interested in a relationship or getting married or having kids. No doubt that was all true. He'd never met a woman that had made him even consider taking that long walk down the aisle.

But he'd never met a woman like Raina before, either. From the moment he'd picked her up at the airport two days ago, something had felt different with her. Something that went beyond a beautiful face and killer body. He'd been drawn to her in a way he never had to another woman before. He still was, dammit.

Those feelings aside, at the moment he'd like to wring her neck. If he had stayed at Gabe's house one minute longer, he just might have.

He knew he'd have to explain everything to his family soon. No doubt they were more than aware that something was up, something big. But he'd needed some time to calm down, to sort out his feelings and think everything through. No one would have wanted to be around him these past two hours.

So he'd come here and pounded on nails. He felt a little calmer now, more clear-headed. He still had no idea how to handle this, or exactly what to say, but he and Raina were going to talk.

Emma was his daughter, his child, and no Sinclair ever walked away from blood.

"He'll be back, Rae. He just needs a little time." Melanie turned off the gas under the teapot on the stove, then poured the hot water into a cup. "Now will you please stop pacing and sit down?"

"It's been over two hours." Raina glanced at her wristwatch and kept moving between the back door and the kitchen sink. "Emma will be waking up from her nap any time now. I don't want him storming in here and frightening her."

"He won't do that." Melanie dropped a tea bag into the cup, then set it on the table. "But I promise you, I'll hit him myself with a frying pan if he does. Now sit."

Reluctantly Raina sat, but she was wound up tighter than Tigger on caffeine. This waiting was making her insane.

She'd never been more embarrassed in her entire

life, facing Lucian's family after they'd heard her tell him that Emma was his baby. If Reese hadn't broken that awful silence, she wasn't certain what she would have done. But everyone had spoken at once after that, and she'd been so overwhelmed, she could barely get a word in.

She'd been thankful, at least, that Gabe had taken Kevin outside right after Lucian's loaded question regarding Emma's parentage. Since the six-year-old hadn't said anything, it didn't seem as though he'd understood what had happened. The rest of the family, however, had fully understood.

The men had held back, a little uncertain what to say or do, but Abby, Sydney, Cara and Melanie had all hugged her. In spite of the circumstances, they all seemed thrilled to have an addition to the family. There'd been no recriminations, no judgments or verdicts handed out. Raina had seen the questions in their eyes, but they hadn't asked. They'd simply accepted.

The Sinclairs were an amazing bunch, Raina had thought as she'd gone back upstairs to lay Emma down for her nap. Truly amazing. By the time Raina had finally gotten Emma to sleep, they'd all cleared out, leaving her alone in the house with Melanie, who'd been fussing over her ever since.

It had taken a while, but Raina had finally told Melanie the truth. Other than the personal details of the night she'd spent with Lucian, she'd explained everything that had happened.

"Drink," Melanie said as she sat in the chair opposite Raina. "You're white as a sheet."

To give her restless hands something to do, Raina picked up the cup Melanie had set down in front of her. The heat felt good on her ice-cold hands, and she sipped the citrusy herbal tea.

"I'm sorry, Mel." Raina stared at the steam rising from her cup. "The last thing I'd ever want to do is upset you."

"Rae, I swear, if you apologize one more time, I just may have to hurt you."

"An empty threat, Mrs. Sinclair." Raina smiled. "We both know you've never hurt anyone in your entire life."

"Not true. Didn't I trip that bully Willie Thomas in seventh grade when he teased Mitsy Davidson for wearing thick glasses?"

"No. *I* tripped him," Raina reminded her.

"Well, it was my idea." Melanie lifted an indignant brow. "You were just closer."

Raina laughed at the memory, then sighed heavily. "Oh, Mel. I was going to tell you about Lucian and me, but I never intended for you to find out quite like this. I came here for your baby shower, not to bring you and your family grief."

"Sweetie, how can you look at your beautiful little girl and think that she could ever bring grief?"

Raina blinked back the moisture in her eyes. "She is beautiful, isn't she?"

"She most certainly is." Melanie smiled, then leaned back, her gaze thoughtful as she looked at Raina. "I did suspect, you know. About you and Lucian."

Raina's head snapped up. "You suspected? But how could you have?"

"I'd been so consumed with Gabe and Kevin and everything that had happened in those months before

I came to Bloomfield that I didn't see it at the wedding," Melanie said. "But when I saw you and Lucian together the other day, saw the way you looked at him, I knew there was something you weren't telling me. Something important that was troubling you deeply."

"Was I really that obvious?"

"Maybe not to anyone else. But you and I have been through a lot together, Rae. I know you better than you know yourself. And it was obvious that Lucian was more than a little interested in you, too."

"But still—" Raina shook her head "—that wouldn't mean that I, that we..." She still couldn't say it out loud to Melanie. "And it certainly wouldn't mean that Emma was Lucian's child."

Melanie smiled. "Like Lucian said, it didn't take a rocket scientist to figure it out. He was just a little slower with the calculations than I was. And let's face it. Emma looks like a Sinclair. Those eyes of hers alone would be enough to make a person wonder. And there was one other thing, something that confused me until today."

"What?"

"You changed the sheets and made up the bed you'd slept in when you stayed with me before. No one has slept in that room since then, so I thought I should freshen the bed before you got here two days ago." She pulled a slip of paper out of the pocket of her dress. "I found this."

Raina looked at the small piece of paper Melanie handed her:

"I'll be right back. Please don't leave. Lucian."

It felt as if the air had been sucked from her lungs.

He'd left a note? All this time she'd thought he'd left without a word.

She couldn't move, couldn't breathe. From the backyard, she heard the sound of Kevin's laughter as he played ball with Gabe and the distant moo of the neighboring farm's cows. The only sound she heard inside was the fierce pounding of her heart.

"I'll be right back."

He'd intended to come back? The words in front of her started to blur, and she blinked to bring them back into focus.

"Please don't leave."

What did that mean? Don't leave before I get back? Or could it have meant don't leave at all?

Her fingers shook. No. Of course it hadn't meant that. It was foolish to read more into a simple note than what was there.

What mattered was that he *had* left a note. That maybe she had meant more to him than a simple, one-night stand.

"I was asleep when he left," Raina whispered hoarsely. "I never saw this."

"It fell between the mattress and headboard. Apparently it's been there all this time." Melanie leaned forward and took Raina's hand. "Oh, Rae. If only you'd told me sooner. What you must have gone through, and all by yourself."

"Emma was worth every minute, every second." Raina closed her eyes. "You never really know until you hold your baby in your arms what it feels like. Nothing else in the world matters. Just that tiny little bundle. You know that you can survive anything as long as you have your child close."

"Can I see that?"

Raina jumped at the sound of Lucian's voice from the kitchen doorway. His denim shirt and jeans were streaked with dirt, his dark hair sprinkled with sawdust. He moved toward her and took the note from her hands, then stared at it. Slowly his dark-green gaze lifted to hers.

"Well—" Melanie stood, glanced from Raina to Lucian "—well, ah, you two obviously need to, ah…talk. I'll go upstairs and check on Emma."

"Melanie, you don't have—"

"Thanks, Mel." Lucian cut her off. "We appreciate it."

When Melanie left, Lucian pulled a chair from the table and placed it at an angle beside Raina, then sat.

His closeness overwhelmed her. The earthy scent of fresh-cut pine and pure male assaulted her senses.

"I'm sorry I left like I did."

"Which time?" she asked coolly.

A muscle jumped in his jaw, and he leaned close. "I just spent the past two hours pounding on nails so that you and I could talk calmly. But I assure you, Raina, I am anything but calm at the moment."

"I'm sorry. You didn't deserve that. I'm a little tense," she admitted. "This is difficult for both of us."

"I'd say that's a bit of an understatement." He sighed heavily, then glanced down at the note in his hand. "I need to know what happened that night."

I fell in love with you, she wanted to say. But she wouldn't. That wasn't what he was asking, or what he wanted to hear.

"We unloaded the presents," she said quietly. "It

had started to snow and I asked you if you wanted some coffee. You said sure, then we both just stood there looking at each other. The next thing I knew I was…we were—'' her cheeks warmed as she hesitated ''—in bed.''

"Of all the things I'm surprised about," he said, and leaned closer still, "it's not that."

The husky tone of his voice and his knees touching her thighs made it difficult for her to think. There was no question that the physical attraction between them was incredibly strong. Which was exactly the reason that she'd kept her distance from the moment she'd met him. Why she needed to keep her distance from him now.

"Raina." He held her with his gaze. "Whatever I've done in my life, I've never been careless when it came to sex. I can't believe we spent an entire night together and we didn't use protection."

The heat on her cheeks turned to fire now. She knew that these questions would come up and that she'd have to answer them, but that didn't make it any easier.

"Of course we did." She folded her hands between her legs and looked down. "But we must have, well, it was more than…" She closed her eyes. "It was a long night, Lucian. I can only guess that one time we might not have been as careful as the others."

"I see."

She couldn't bring herself to look at him, didn't want to see the regret she was certain would be in his eyes. Because no matter what happened now, she would never regret that night or the beautiful child it had brought her.

So she kept talking, kept her voice level and controlled.

"The next couple of months I attributed my exhaustion to the move and the long hours I was putting in at work. By the third month I knew something wasn't right. A drugstore pregnancy test confirmed my suspicions."

"And you called me?"

She nodded. "I admit I was afraid, but I thought you should know."

"Until I said, 'Raina who?'" he added with a sigh.

"Yes."

He said nothing for a long moment, then he stood and walked to the kitchen sink, turned and faced her. His expression was somber, his mouth pressed into a hard line.

"As I see it," he said tightly, "there's only one solution to our problem."

Confused, she looked at him.

"We're getting married."

Six

Lucian watched Raina's expression leap from confused to shocked. He'd expected that. Hell, no one could be more shocked than him.

"*What* did you say?"

"We can get a license in the morning, have our blood tests done right after that, then as soon as the state allows, we can go see a justice of the peace."

She stared at him as if he'd grown a second nose. "You hit yourself in the head with that hammer, right? Or maybe that accident you had after the wedding did more to your brain than just lose you a few hours."

He'd expected reluctance, but he certainly hadn't expected sarcasm. "Look, I realize this is catching you off guard. I admit the idea took some getting used to, but if you think about it, you'll see it's the only sensible thing to do."

"If I *think* about it?"

"That's right."

"The *only* sensible thing to do?"

Why the hell did she keep repeating what he'd said? "Yes."

She turned away from him then and dropped her head in her hands. When her shoulders started to shake, he moved toward her. Good Lord, he hadn't meant to make her cry.

"Raina, it's for the best, we have Emma to think about and—" He stopped suddenly, narrowed his eyes. "Are you *laughing?*"

She lifted her head and waved a hand to signal she needed a moment, but a fresh round of laughter seemed to grip her and her head dropped back down again.

Folding his arms, he said through clenched teeth, "Are you just about finished?"

She visibly struggled to compose herself, then stood and faced him, still wiping tears from the corner of her eyes. "You think marrying you would be the *sensible* thing to do? That's got to be the most ridiculous thing I've ever heard."

"Oh, is that so?" He took a step closer to her. "And just why is our getting married so ridiculous?"

"This is the twenty-first century, Sinclair. Shotgun weddings are retrograde."

"No one's putting a gun to my head, dammit. Emma is my daughter, and I'm trying to do what's right."

"We can do what's right without getting married, for heaven's sake. We'll work this out, Lucian. It's not necessary for you to make the supreme sacrifice here.''

"Who the hell said it was a supreme sacrifice?" he yelled. "If you'd just—"

The sound of Emma's quiet whimper came through the baby monitor, then Melanie's soft croon. Raina pressed her lips together and narrowed her eyes, then moved so close they were nearly nose-to-nose.

"For the first ten years of my life," she said tightly, "I lived with parents who were vocal enough about their dislike of each other that my family was on a first-name basis with the police. I understand you're angry about this. But I won't tolerate shouting when my daughter is in the same house, do you understand that?"

Frustrated, he stared down at her, then sighed heavily and dragged a hand through his hair. "Look, I'm still trying to find my balance here. Whatever you might think of me, having a kid, being a father, is not something I take lightly. Emma is not just your daughter. She's mine, too. That means something to me, dammit."

Slowly the tension eased from her face and her shoulders relaxed. "Lucian," she said softly, "I admit when I came here two days ago I might have thought you were less than admirable. If I had known you'd left a note or that you'd had an accident, things might have been different. But the fact is, that *is* what happened then, and this is now. Now is what we have to deal with."

"Fine. I'll accept that," he said evenly. "Now give me one good reason why we shouldn't get married."

Exasperation rumbled deep in her throat. "Have

you listened to a thing I've said here? I could give you a dozen reasons.''

''Are you living with someone?''

''Of course not.''

''Dating someone?''

''Not seriously.''

''Well, neither am I.''

She stared at him in disbelief. ''And you think that because neither one of us is involved with anyone else at the moment that we should get married?''

''No, I think we should get married because we have a child. I don't want anyone to ever point a finger at our daughter or whisper behind her back.''

She faltered, then squared her shoulders. ''Single women, and men, raise children all the time now.''

She'd tried to hide it, but he'd seen the fleeting pain, the concern, in her smoky-blue eyes. And her voice hadn't been quite so strong or so sure. ''And I applaud them as well as respect them. But there are small minds out there. There always will be. Do we want our daughter to be a target for them?''

She turned away, rubbed at her arms. ''My friends, the people I know, aren't like that. I would never let anyone hurt her.''

''There'll be kids at school, maybe the people who live next door or the clerk at the grocery store. Just one comment, even an innocent one, could hurt her. Let me protect her from that.'' He moved up behind her, put his hands on her shoulders. ''Emma's my daughter, Raina. While she's still a baby, let me give her my name.''

She shook her head, but didn't move away. ''We don't love each other, Lucian. What kind of marriage is it when two people barely know each other and have nothing in common?''

"We can get to know each other.'' He felt the heat of her skin through her soft cotton blouse, smelled the faint floral scent of her perfume. "And we obviously do have something in common.''

"So like a man.'' Ice edged her words as she turned and stepped back. "This isn't about sex, Lucian. This is about Emma.''

"I was talking about Emma.''

"Oh.'' She shifted awkwardly. "Well, good.''

"But since you brought the subject up—'' he closed the space she'd put between them ''—let's talk about that.''

"There's nothing to talk about.''

"Isn't there?''

"Get over yourself, Sinclair.'' Her chin lifted. "It was one night.''

He smiled, watched her eyes darken to the color of thick, blue smoke when he touched a finger to the collar of her blouse. Desire sparked, then flared bright. "Was it just one night?'' he murmured. "Or was it something more?''

With the tip of his finger, he followed the open V of her collar down and circled the first white button. His gaze dropped to her mouth. Her lips parted softly and her breathing turned shallow.

"Something tells me that's what happened the first time,'' he said thoughtfully. "That you, maybe we both, denied it, until it just sort of exploded between us. Am I right?''

"No.'' The single word was breathless, edged with panic.

He lowered his mouth within a breath of hers, hovered there. "I think that's a lie, Raina," he whispered.

She blinked, did not move toward him or away. "No, Lucian. That's what a marriage between us would be. A lie."

He closed his eyes on a sigh and stepped back. "Dammit, it wouldn't be like that. We could—"

"No." She shook her head adamantly. "We can't. I'm going to be here for another four days." Her voice softened. "I want to be as fair as possible with you. You're welcome to spend as much time with Emma as you want. We can figure out some kind of visitation schedule before I leave, if you'd like to. I'm hoping we'll be able to do this without lawyers."

Visitation schedule? *Lawyers?* He wanted to tell her *exactly* what he thought of that, but there were times when he knew it was best to keep his mouth shut. "Fine," he snapped out.

"I'm going to check on Emma now." When she moved to step around him, he caught hold of her arm.

"I lost seven whole months of my daughter's life, Raina." He pulled her up against him. "Just tell me this, how *fair* is that?"

"I'm sorry, Lucian," she said quietly, and he could see that she meant it.

He swore silently, then let her go. He stared at the closed door for a long moment after she was gone, struggled not to follow her.

Damn stubborn woman.

She might have won the first round, he thought irritably, but round two would be coming soon. Very soon.

He intended to be ready.

* * *

"Look, sweetie," Melanie cooed to Emma when Raina walked into the nursery. "There's your mommy now."

"I can do that." Raina moved beside the changing table where Emma smiled and kicked her feet at the sight of her mother. "Hello, my darling. Did you have a nice nap?"

Her daughter's smile got her every time, Raina thought. Made her heart swell, her throat thicken. Made the stress of the day disappear, no matter how bad it was.

She desperately needed that smile at this moment.

Melanie handed Raina a diaper and raised one brow. "Well?"

"Well…" Raina slipped the diaper under her daughter and smoothly taped the sides. "He, ah, thinks that we should get married."

"He thinks *what?*"

"That we should get married." It surprised Raina how calm her voice sounded when inside she was still shaking. "Would you hand me that little pink T-shirt on top of the diaper bag, please?"

"Let me get this straight." Eyes wide, Melanie stared at her. "Lucian Sinclair, my brother-in-law, a man who cherishes his bachelor of bachelor arts degree, asked you to marry him and you say, 'hand me that T-shirt'?"

"Well, actually, to be more specific—" Raina took the T-shirt from Melanie "—I said 'hand me that little pink T-shirt.'"

"Raina, for heaven's sake. What did you say?"

"I said no."

"Well, of course you did." Melanie furrowed her brow. "What in the world was he thinking?"

"He was thinking of Emma." With a fresh diaper and change of clothes, Raina kissed her daughter, then picked her up and cuddled. "He wants her to have his name. To protect her from small-minded people."

Melanie frowned. "Small-minded people?"

Raina kissed the silky top of Emma's head and breathed in the baby scent of her soft skin. "People with mean spirits and ugly thoughts who are just looking for a reason to gossip."

"Lord knows I've met more than a few of them myself," Melanie said with a sigh. "But still, marriage?"

"In theory it makes sense." Just the thought of those kind of people had Raina clenching her teeth. "It was the one thing, probably the only thing, that he could have said to make me even consider such a ridiculous idea."

"Are you saying that you *are* considering his proposal?"

"Of course not." Raina shook her head firmly, but even she could hear the doubt in her voice. What if Lucian was right? What if people did point or whisper behind Emma's back? Even considering the possibility made her chest hurt. "I told him that he could spend as much time with Emma as he wants, and that we'd work out a visitation schedule."

"Oh, good heavens." Melanie's eyes went wide. "I can just imagine how well *that* went over."

"There was a significant amount of chest thumping." Raina nibbled on the finger that Emma was attempting to stick in her mouth. "But he agreed."

"Don't be so sure, Rae." Doubt narrowed Melanie's eyes. "The Sinclair men can be quite persuasive when they set their minds to something. Believe me, I know."

"It's different with you and Gabe," Raina said firmly. "You love each other. Lucian and I barely like each other."

Melanie laughed. "Right. You just keep telling yourself that, honey. Who knows, maybe you'll even start to believe it."

At the sound of Kevin's voice calling her from downstairs, Melanie headed for the door. "I've got to get down there before my son and husband decide that a snack before dinner means a piece of cake the size of a Volkswagen. Come down and join us when you're ready."

Raina frowned as she shifted her daughter from one hip to the other. She could resist Lucian Sinclair. She could.

But she *had* felt a moment of weakness in the kitchen. When he'd slid the tip of his finger over her collar down to the button of her shirt. And when he'd brought his mouth to within a whisper of hers. Her skin had felt tight and hot, her breasts had tingled. An image of another time, when he'd kissed her hard and long, when he'd touched her all over, had sprung into her mind. And she'd wanted his mouth on hers, his hands on her body again.

He was right. She had lied. That night had been everything he'd said. They'd denied themselves until they'd exploded with need for each other. It was the most powerful experience of her life, the most incredible.

And the worst of it was, she thought in despair, that it was still there. The building of tension under the surface, threatening to erupt once again if she wasn't careful.

I'll be careful, she resolved, and followed Melanie out of the room. She hesitated at the deep sound of Lucian's voice, realized that he hadn't left. Her pulse skipped.

Very, very careful, she told herself.

With a deep breath she squared her shoulders and moved down the stairs.

It was one thing to tickle and play peekaboo with a baby and quite another to give it a bath and change its diaper.

Sheer panic filled Lucian as he stared down at the squirming, half-naked baby he'd just laid down on the changing table. Good Lord, he'd felt less fear the first time he'd jumped out of an airplane to skydive.

He must have been insane to insist that Raina let him take over after she'd put Emma in the tub for her bath. He'd seen the worry in Raina's eyes, had reassured her he was more than capable. After all, how difficult could it be? he'd thought. He'd seen Cara give Matthew a bath before. She'd made it look easy enough.

About as easy as climbing a greased rope.

He had managed to get one arm into the tiny, white T-shirt, but Emma wouldn't quite cooperate with the second arm. And something was definitely wrong with the diaper he'd put on, though he wasn't sure what.

"Need some help?" Raina asked from behind him.

He glanced over his shoulder at her, saw her watching him from the doorway, a bottle in her hand. Her eyes held a mixture of amusement and concern.

"I got it." He managed to get the second arm in the T-shirt and felt a surge of pride.

"It's on backward," she said, moving closer.

"I know how to put a T-shirt on," he defended. "I do it every day. Tag goes in the back."

"I was talking about the diaper."

"Oh." He glanced down. So *that* was the problem.

"And it really would be easier if you put the T-shirt over her head before you try stuffing her arms in. She has a sweet temperament, but it can only be stretched so far."

There comes a time in every man's life when he has to admit defeat, Lucian thought in resignation. This was definitely one of those times.

"I would have figured it out," he muttered, but stepped to the side and let Raina move beside him.

"Yeah, but ten-year-olds don't wear diapers," she replied sweetly.

"Ha, ha." He blew a shock of hair from his forehead. "I would have had it down pat by age two, no later than three."

He watched Raina's slender fingers move swiftly to repair the damage he'd done with both the diaper and T-shirt. When she reached for the pajamas, he knew he couldn't have managed without reinforcements. Emma would have been traumatized for life if he'd attempted putting that garment on her.

"So she has my personality, does she?" he asked while Raina slipped Emma's foot into the soft fleece sleeper.

She glanced up at him, confused.

"You said she has a sweet temperament."

At his comment Emma pressed her lips together and made a wet, razzing sound, then softly burped.

"Well, there are one or two similarities, I suppose," Raina said with a smirk.

When Emma started to babble, Lucian couldn't hold back a grin. Seemed that he'd been doing a lot of that today, at least every time he looked at his daughter.

His *daughter*.

The words themselves were still foreign to him, but somehow Emma wasn't. He'd stayed for dinner, then he and Emma had spent the evening playing on the living room floor. He'd been around babies before and he'd thought they were pretty cute, but he'd never been mesmerized. Everything that Emma did fascinated him. From reaching for a rattle to trying to sit up by herself, he'd thought the child was brilliant.

"Time for night-night, sweetie." Raina picked Emma up and nuzzled her cheek, then reached for the bottle.

"Will she let me?" Lucian asked.

"I'm not sure. She's never had a man give her a bottle at bedtime before."

Those words gave Lucian tremendous pleasure. He hated the possibility that some guy might have held his daughter this way. It was strange to him that he'd known for fewer than twelve hours that he was a father, yet he already felt extremely possessive of his child.

And his child's mother, as well.

He didn't like the idea that another man would be there at bedtime—Emma's *or* Raina's.

She handed him the baby first, then the bottle. "Sit over here in the rocker."

After a moment of fidgeting on both their sides, Lucian settled into the rocking chair with Emma. Her little hands opened and closed on the bottle, and she made soft, mewling sounds as she happily drank her bedtime formula. All the while, her bright green eyes stayed on him.

Raina shut off the overhead light, then turned on the Winnie the Pooh lamp on the dresser. "She should fall asleep before she finishes the bottle," Raina said quietly as she walked backward toward the door. "Lay her on her back and cover her with the blanket in the crib."

"Raina, stay." Lucian nodded toward a step stool sitting beside the rocker. "Come sit with us. Tell me about Emma."

She hesitated, then moved beside him and sat. "What would you like to know?"

"Everything." He looked down at the baby, saw her eyelids growing heavy. "How much did she weigh? What does she like? Does she sleep through the night? Is she healthy? What do you—"

"Whoa, wait up." Raina put up a hand to stop him. "One question at a time."

With Emma asleep in his arms, they sat there in the dim light while Raina answered each question he asked. He chuckled when she told him how Emma made a face the first time she'd eaten peas, he frowned when he heard that she'd had an allergic reaction to an antibiotic for an ear infection. How he wished he'd been there for all of that, for every first. The first smile, the first laugh, the first bite of food.

Every question she answered, every story she told, made Emma more his than before, made those two words, *his baby*, more of a reality.

By the time he laid her in her crib, with Raina standing beside him, he knew that there was no going back. Emma was his child, his daughter.

She was going to have his name.

Seven

"Hold it. Right there. No, wait, move to your left."

Raina held back the groan hovering deep in her throat and shifted to the left.

"Wait, wait, stop right there. That's it, that's it. Now smile."

She swore she might scream if she heard that word one more time. But she smiled anyway. Whatever it took to get this over with as quickly as possible.

A brand-new father with a brand-new camera was a force to be reckoned with.

Lucian had shown up at Gabe and Melanie's doorstep an hour ago and dragged her and Emma out into the backyard, spread a blanket on the sun-warmed grass with a few of the new baby toys he'd bought over the past two days, then started shooting pictures. He'd gone through at least four rolls of film so far, crawled on his stomach and practically stood on his head while he busily snapped the shutter. There were grass marks on his faded jeans, smudges of dirt on his navy-blue T-shirt and fragments of twigs and spring leaves in his dark hair. And still his enthusiasm had not yet dimmed in the slightest.

Raina might not have minded the impromptu photo shoot so much if Lucian hadn't insisted she be in the pictures, too. She'd tried arguing that it wasn't necessary for her to be included, that dressed in a white cotton tank top and jeans she would look out of place against the pretty pink dress Emma wore. She'd even tried to get him to let her take the pictures, contended that it made more sense for him to be in the photos, not her.

But tenacity seemed to be the man's middle name. He wouldn't let her change her clothes or take even one picture. If there was one thing to be said about Lucian Sinclair, Raina thought, it was his capacity to throw himself completely into whatever it was he set his mind to do.

She respected that attribute as much as she feared it.

In the past two days, since their discussion about marriage, he hadn't once brought the subject up again. He hadn't said anything to her about visitations or schedules or what was going to happen after she and Emma left the day after tomorrow. He'd simply played endlessly with his daughter, asked every conceivable question about her life for the past seven months and even insisted on dressing and bathing her. While part of Raina felt relieved, part of her was suspicious. He was making this easy, Raina thought.

Too easy.

And *that* made her nervous.

"Perfect." Lucian hunkered down at the edge of the blanket, smiled at his daughter while he shook a waggle-eared stuffed dog named Blue. It was one of at least six stuffed animals he'd bought for Emma and it seemed to be her favorite. "Let's get a shot with her holding Blue."

"We did that shot already," Raina informed him dryly. "Five or six times, I believe. We should go in now."

"Why?" He reached for a new roll of film. "Blue skies, a few clouds in the distance, warm breeze. Emma's having a good time. What could be better than this?"

That was the problem. She couldn't think of anything better. And Emma wasn't the only one having a good time, Raina thought. *She* was having a good time, too. And that was a dangerous thing. The more time she spent with Lucian, the harder it was going to be to leave.

The harder it was to keep her hands off him.

He'd been a perfect gentleman with her these past two days, charming and funny, asked questions about the fashion business and exactly what it was that she did. He never mentioned the night they'd made love or asked questions, made no sexual advances toward her or even showed more interest in her than he probably did any other woman.

He confused the hell out of her.

He frustrated the hell out of her.

Every time he got close to her, every innocent brush of their shoulders or hands, turned her insides soft and warm. All he had to do was look at her with those eyes of his, smile at her with that intoxicating Sinclair smile, and her knees went weak.

He grinned at her now, and she was glad that she was sitting with Emma in her lap. That's all it took, just a look, and she was lost.

"What?" she asked a little more sharply than she'd intended.

He sat on the blanket beside her, stretched out those long, muscular legs of his and pulled Emma onto his knees. "I was just wondering if you used to be this difficult when you were posing for all those magazine ads."

She rolled her eyes. "Mister, if you think *I'm* difficult, come backstage to one of my shows sometime. Those girls give new meaning to the word *difficult*. And anyway—" she lifted her hair off her neck, enjoyed the feel of the cool breeze on her warm skin "—that was a long time ago."

"Why did you quit?" Lucian asked. "All that fame and glamour?"

She couldn't help but laugh at that. "Eight hours in a bikini, posing on top of a mountain where it's thirty degrees and the wind is blowing, or six hours in one-hundred-degree heat dressed in heavy hiking gear is about as far from glamorous as you can get."

Smiling, he bounced Emma on his knee and made her laugh. "Melanie said that if you'd stayed with it, the name Raina would have been as recognized as Naomi or Cindy or Christy. She said you were known for 'The Look.'"

"Melanie's my friend. She feels obligated to say that." She glanced away, plucked a small yellow flower from the lawn, then tickled her daughter's cheek with it. "And as far as 'The Look' goes, my entire career was based on three of them."

"Yeah?" He gathered Emma into his lap and picked up his camera. "Let me see them."

"Oh, no." She put out a hand and shook her head.

"Tell Mommy I'll stop taking pictures if she co-operates," Lucian said to Emma.

"Promise?"

"Promise."

"All right, then, here goes. This is the 'Who, me?' look. I just imagine I've won the lottery." She cocked her head, lifted her brows and pursed her lips in surprise. Lucian snapped the pose, then she stared blankly into the camera. "This is the 'I don't have a thought in my brain' look. I just think of what's inside a balloon."

He laughed as he snapped another picture. Emma stuck a rattle in her mouth and cooed.

"And this is the 'Come take me, I'm yours,' look." She dipped her head, glanced upward as she parted her lips. "I imagine I'm about to be kissed by—"

You.

He glanced over his camera at her. "By who?"

She felt her cheeks flush. "Ah...Harry Connick Jr."

"Harry Connick Jr.?" He looked at her doubtfully.

She nodded. "I'm crazy about Harry."

Shaking his head, he raised his camera again. "Don't move."

Her gaze drifted to Lucian's mouth, and she couldn't help but remember what wonderful things he could do with that mouth. The breeze skimmed over her warm skin; the sweet scent of spring hyacinths filled the air. And all she could think was how much she wanted to touch his lips with her own, felt herself leaning toward him....

"Hello. Anybody out here?"

Raina jumped at the sound of Melanie's voice from the back porch. She and Gabe had left for a doctor's appointment before Lucian had showed up at the house this morning. Apparently, they had returned.

"Out here," Lucian called, then turned and took a picture of Gabe and Melanie as they crossed the lawn.

Gabe scooped Emma up into his arms. Emma squealed with pleasure, and Lucian took another shot.

"Uh-oh." Melanie looked at the camera. "Looks like somebody bought himself a toy today."

"How was your appointment?" Raina asked.

"The doctor said everything's fine." Melanie smoothed her hands lovingly over her belly and smiled. "Won't be too much longer."

"Don't see how it could be," Gabe said. "If she gets any bigger, I'm going to have to widen the doorways."

"Why do you think I married you?" Melanie cocked her head and looked at her husband. "A woman never knows when she'll need a good carpenter or mechanic. Since Bill at the garage was already married, that left me with you."

"And here I thought you married me for my good looks and sense of humor," Gabe said with a wounded-puppy-dog look.

"Shoot, she would have married *me* if she wanted those things," Lucian quipped, then snapped another picture when Gabe glared at him.

"Come on, cutie-pie." Melanie enticed the baby from Gabe and headed for the house. "Emma and I are hungry, aren't we?"

"I think there's a side of beef in the outside freezer," Gabe teased as he followed his wife, then played innocent when Melanie shot him a look over her shoulder. Shaking her head, Raina started to rise.

"Wait." Lucian took hold of her arm once Gabe and Melanie were out of earshot.

"You promised no more pictures," she said firmly.

"I want to talk to you."

Her pulse picked up speed. She glanced down at his hand on her arm, felt the sizzle of his touch all the way to her toes. "About?"

"You know."

All morning there'd been a playfulness in his eyes and manner. But not now. Now his eyes were intent, his manner somber.

"All right." She settled back. "Go ahead."

"Not here, Raina." He kept those forest-green eyes on her. "We need to go someplace where we can be alone."

Lucian parked his truck and came around to open the door for Raina. He knew she was nervous, though he wasn't certain if she was worried about having a conversation about Emma, or if she was worried about being alone with him.

He suspected it was both.

She'd been quiet on the short drive from Gabe and Melanie's but hadn't asked him where they were going. She'd simply sat opposite him, her shoulders stiff and back rigid as she stared straight ahead, no doubt preparing herself for what she assumed would be the worst.

"Maybe I should call Melanie," Raina said when he opened the truck door. "Just to make sure she got Emma down for her nap all right."

"Emma's fine, Raina. And Gabe's there for the rest of the afternoon, too. So stop worrying."

The furrow on her brow gave way to surprise when she stepped out of the truck and looked up at the framed house. She glanced at him with questioning eyes.

He shrugged. "It's sort of a hobby."

"It's yours?"

"Mine and the bank's, but mostly mine. It doesn't look like much yet, but I'm almost finished with the framing." He took her arm. "Come on, I'll give you the nickel tour."

He'd designed the house himself, a mixture of contemporary and ranch-style, with raised front and back porches and double-wide entry doors that hadn't been set yet. He'd picked them out, though. A pair of oak beauties with beveled glass.

"I'm in between projects now with my company," he said as they moved up the front steps. "I'll get the drywall and windows in next."

"Is that how you work on it? A little here and there when you have the time?"

"Something like that." He paused at the open entry. "After you, madam."

She strolled inside, the sound of her low heels on the bare wooden floors echoing in the cavernous entry and living room. Her jaw went slack. "This is *huge*."

"Four thousand square feet." He grinned at her

sheepishly. "I got a little carried away with the plans."

She moved from the entry to the living room, shaking her head in awe, then went into the kitchen. He watched her face transform into a look of reverence.

"Oh, Lucian." She gasped, hurried to the empty frame where the window above the kitchen sink would be installed, then gasped again. "The view is incredible."

"It is, isn't it?" he said without modesty and came to stand beside her. "The living room, kitchen and master bedroom all have the same view of the woods."

A chilly wind suddenly swept through the open window, lifting the ends of her hair. Outside, thick, puffy clouds surrounded the midday sun. He watched her shiver, then rub her arms as she turned to look at him. "It's beautiful."

You're beautiful, he wanted to say, but knew better. She'd finally let down that carefully guarded wall she'd been hiding behind for the past few days, and he didn't want to spoil the moment. Right now she was looking at him with such pleasure and delight that he felt his chest tighten with need. He wanted desperately to take her in his arms, right here, with the wind in her hair and a chill on her mouth. Wanted to kiss that chill away, to hear his name on her lips and to feel her hands on his skin.

Instead, he jammed his hands into his jeans and just smiled. "Thanks. It's a work in progress, but I'm getting there." He frowned when she shivered again. "We can leave if you're too cold."

She shook her head. "I'm fine. And besides, you

promised the nickel tour, remember? I've still got about three cents left, I'd say.''

He showed her the rest of the downstairs, which included a game room, a room that would be an office and a guest bathroom. Upstairs, there were two more bedrooms with full baths, a loft, plus the master bedroom and bath.

He couldn't help but feel pride as he watched her ooh and ahh over a design feature or compliment him on the work he'd done. Other than the female members of his family, he'd never brought a woman here before. He'd always kept this part of his life separate from the women he'd dated. Raina was the first.

In more than one way, he realized, and the thought sobered him.

He'd spent the past two days with Emma, played with her, actually learned how to change a diaper that stayed put, feed her cereal and bottles and given her a bath. He had no words to describe the feeling in his chest every time he looked at his daughter, but he knew what it was. For the first time in his life, he felt something that went as deep as a feeling can go. Something that quite literally took his breath away, something that scared the hell out of him but made him feel warm and full at the same time.

He loved Emma. Loved her as much as if he'd been there every day with her since she'd been born. He'd missed out on so much already, he didn't want to miss even one more day. He wanted to be a part of her life.

He wanted her to have his name.

He'd given Raina space these past two days, but the clock was quickly ticking the minutes away before they would be back on a plane to New York. He'd spent the past two nights pacing in frustration, wracking his brain for a solution.

He couldn't let them leave, dammit. He *couldn't*.

Because he didn't just want Emma. He wanted Emma's mother, too.

He watched her inspect the large walk-in closet in the master bedroom, heard her squeak of approval over size. So what if it wasn't a conventional marriage? he thought. People married and lived together for reasons other than love. They liked each other— at least, most of the time, anyway. And there was no question they were physically attracted to each other, in spite of Raina's denial. So maybe he hadn't planned on settling down and doing the picket fence, forever thing. He had Emma to think about now. What was important now was what was good for her.

Thunder rattled the open eaves overhead and snapped him out of his wandering thoughts. Rain began to tap on the roof.

"Uh-oh." He took her hand and pulled her from the closet, then headed down the stairs. "We'd better get out of here."

By the time they hit the porch downstairs, the sky had opened up. They were halfway down the porch steps when Lucian heard the sound.

Damn.

"What is it?" she asked over a rumble of thunder.

Shaking his head, he pulled her back up onto the porch, under the eaves. "Stay there for a moment."

While she waited on the porch, he knelt down in the wet dirt and looked under the steps. Water was running underneath.

"Lucian, what is it?"

"There's a litter of kittens under the front porch," he called back. "The mother is wild and won't let me near, but I leave food out, so—hey, wait."

Before he could stop her, she was already down on her hands and knees beside him in the pouring rain. "I see the babies," she said excitedly, "but there's water dripping on them."

"She'll never come out," he yelled over a new crash of thunder. "I'll be right back."

He ran and grabbed a tarp that covered a large stack of concrete mix. He knew every bag would be ruined, but what the hell. So he'd buy more. He was back in one minute, had the steps covered in two.

"Okay." She waved a hand, then stood and grinned at him. "They're dry now."

Shaking his head, he grabbed her hand. They were both muddy and wet, and he knew Raina had to be freezing. "Let's get out of here."

He dragged her behind him about thirty yards through the woods, and they dashed to the thirty-two-foot trailer he'd parked on the property. It wasn't luxurious, but it could hardly be called roughing it, either.

They were both soaked through by the time they ran up the steps, then fell, laughing and gasping, through the door.

"Hold on." He left her shivering and dripping on the small tiled entry, grabbed a towel from a closet and was back in two seconds.

He dropped the towel over her head and scrubbed at her wet hair, then wrapped it around her shoulders.

"That was extremely heroic, Mr. Sinclair." She

wiped at her face. "Who would have guessed you have a soft spot not only for babies, but kittens, too?"

"Don't tell anyone." He raked his soaked hair back from his face. "I do have an image to maintain, you know."

"Ah, yes, your image," she said with a grin, then wiped at his face with the towel. "Tough guy."

Her cheeks were flushed from the run, her eyes bright and sparkling. Her smile faded as their eyes met; her hand stilled.

The towel dropped from her fingers, then cautiously she reached out and touched his cheek with her hand.

His heart slammed in his chest when her gaze dropped to his mouth, and she slowly closed the distance between them.

"Lucian…"

Eight

This is crazy, Raina told herself. Pure insanity mixed with foolishness.

And she just didn't give a damn.

The feel of his cheek under her fingertips was wet but warm, with a slight stubble of beard. They'd brought the scent of the rain in with them, but the storm pounding over their heads on the trailer roof was nothing compared to the storm that pounded inside her body.

"Lucian." She whispered his name again. Water dripped from his hair down his face. When she swept her thumb lightly over his lips to brush the raindrops away, she felt his jaw tighten.

His hand, rough and calloused, closed over her fingers; a glint, something primitive and dangerous and intensely sensual, shone in his narrowed eyes.

"I know this is, that we—"

His mouth slammed against hers, hard and demanding. In one swift move he forced her backward, pinning her body between his and the closed door. Flames of heat licked at her skin and raced through her blood. She clung to him, was certain her knees wouldn't hold her up if she didn't. She tasted the storm on his lips, his tongue, met every thrust of heat with her own.

Fire and rain, she thought, as dazed as she was aroused at the feel of his greedy lips on hers. A tiny voice of reason whispered from somewhere in the back of her mind, but she ignored it. What was happening between her and Lucian had nothing to do with reason. Nothing at all.

This was about pleasure. About a need so strong, so deep, it refused to be denied.

As it had been the first time, she thought. And every time after.

As it was now.

She pressed closer to him, felt the solid wall of his muscled chest, his broad shoulders, the force of his mouth on hers.

The hard proof of his own need for her.

Everything sent her senses spinning, excited her as only Lucian could. He was the only man who had ever made her feel this way, made her completely lose control, released a passion inside her that she'd never known existed.

A moment of despair filled her as she realized that he was the only man who *could* bring her to this, that even if he didn't love her, he would still be the only man.

Then he cupped her buttocks and lifted her against him, fitted her rain-drenched body to his, and she had no more thoughts other than him.

"Raina." He yanked his mouth from hers, dragged his lips across her jaw, then down her throat. "Tell me you want me as much as I do you."

Because she couldn't find her breath, she simply moaned and pressed closer.

He held back, brought his face up to look into her eyes. "You need to say it. I need to hear you say you want me."

She stared at him in bewilderment. How could he question such a thing? Maybe she hadn't come out and said it, but she was the one who'd instigated this, the one who'd practically begged him to take her.

"Say it," he repeated, his voice husky and strained. "I need you to say it."

"I want you, Lucian." She took his face in her hands. "You know I've wanted you from the first time I saw you."

He stared at her, his eyes the color of the woods outside. She felt a moment of fear, a fear of entering the uncertainty of that dark, deep forest, certain that she'd be lost there forever.

But it was too late to turn back, she knew. She was already hopelessly lost.

Once again she brought her mouth to his, gently this time, kissed him as she'd never kissed another man. With her lips, her heart, her soul.

The heat built again; every brush of her lips, every tiny nip of teeth, every soft, delicate slide of her tongue against his, stoked the flames of desire. The need grew restless, rattled at the lock of its cage and screamed to be released.

"Raina." His incredible, magical mouth moved down her neck again, teasing, tasting. "Wrap your legs around me."

She did, then groaned at the fire-hot feel of his lips nibbling below her earlobe. This was everything she'd remembered, everything she'd dreamed about since that night so long ago.

Everything and more.

"Put your head on my shoulder," he whispered as he tightly circled her with his arms and carried her. The ceiling was low, and when he moved toward a small bedroom to the right, he had to duck his head to clear the doorway.

He stood at the foot of his bed, still holding her, both of them oblivious to their rain-soaked clothes and hair. She grasped his head in her hands, brought her lips to his, not gently this time, but ruthlessly.

His tongue mated, swirled with hers; his strong arms held her. Struggling for breath, she pulled back, met his moss-green gaze with her own as she dragged her wet tank top over her head and tossed it down on the floor at the foot of the bed. A fierce, feral look glinted in his eyes as he looked at her.

And then he feasted.

His mouth closed over the tip of her breast, nipped through damp, white lace, then suckled. She gasped at the arrow of pleasure that shot through her.

While his mouth and teeth worked magic on her, she clasped his head and brought him closer still, raked her fingers through his scalp as she bit her lip to keep from crying out.

"Take this off," he murmured.

Her fingers shook as she unsnapped the front catch of her bra. His mouth was on her bare flesh before she could slip the straps from her shoulders; his tongue found her pebbled nipple even as the lace garment dropped to the floor. White-hot pleasure rippled through her body as he kneaded and caressed her breast with his mouth, his lips, his teeth.

And his tongue…oh, heavens…what he was doing to her.

He blazed kisses over the swell of one breast to the other. Again and again he assaulted her senses: flames of heat licked her body; cold shimmered over her still-damp skin; blood pounded in her temples and drowned out everything but the sound of her own soft cries and the sudden crash of thunder.

"Was that outside or in here?" she asked raggedly.

He chuckled, then whispered, "Put your arms around me and hang on."

She did, and his mouth caught her gasp as they fell backward onto the bed with her on top of him. Another clap of thunder shook the trailer and they rolled with it, clung to each other as the storm raged on.

"Your shirt." She was already tugging at the damp fabric. He yanked it off.

Shoes came next; they both alternately swore and laughed in the struggle to remove wet jeans.

And then they were bare skin to bare skin, mouth to mouth. The urgency built within even as the storm raged outside. Her body throbbed with need, a sweet ache that coiled tightly between her legs, increasing with every stroke of his hand, every brush of his lips, every nip of his teeth.

There was nothing gentle about his touch. He plundered and ravaged, and all she could think was *more*.

"Wait." His voice was raw as he jerked his mouth from hers. He rolled away for what felt like a lifetime, but it was only a few seconds. When he turned back to her, he dragged her close, then pulled her underneath him.

The storm was in his eyes now, a wild, crashing, deep-green sea of passion. She arched toward him, gave herself up to the waves, felt herself rising up with the crest.

"You're beautiful," he murmured as he gazed down at her, knew that the words sounded trite. He knew that she'd heard them hundreds of times. When she reached for him, he shook his head in frustration.

He wanted her to know, to understand, that she was special. That *this* was special.

"I'll always remember you like this," he said. "No matter what happens, I'll always remember."

Her eyes, glazed with desire, held his. She smiled softly. "So will I," she whispered. "So will I."

He linked hands with her then, raised her arms over her head, entered her slowly. Her lips parted, her eyes closed while her breasts rose and fell sharply.

When at last he was deep inside her, she whimpered softly and moved her hips upward.

"Lucian," she gasped his name. "Please."

With their hands still intertwined, he started to move. She murmured encouragement, a disjointed mix of pleasure and soft moans. Her head rolled from side to side, her body bowed.

"Let me touch you." Her voice was urgent, demanding. "I need to touch you."

He released her and she reached for him, scraped her fingernails over his shoulders as her arms hauled him closer. Her lips sought his and took possession of his mouth. When he slid his hands down to her hips and gripped her tightly to him, a soft moan rose from deep in her throat. His heart beat as wild and fierce as the storm that was now overhead.

"Open your eyes." He dragged his mouth from hers. "Look at me."

Her eyelids slowly fluttered open and through a thick haze of desire, she met his gaze.

"Lucian." His name was a breathless whisper of need on her kiss-swollen lips. "Lucian," she repeated. "Now, please."

Her soft plea nearly sent him to the edge, but still he held back. His skin was no longer damp from the rain, but from sweat as he struggled to prolong the intense sensations exploding in his body. Sensations that increased with every thrust of his hips, with every sweep of her restless hands.

Blinding need drove him on, until, like that first distant sound of thunder, he felt the shudder roll from her body into his. Crying out, she clutched at him. He shuddered with her, bodies entwined, and they tumbled over the edge together.

The rain settled to a soft drumming on the trailer roof. Under the comfort of a blue cotton blanket, Raina nestled in the crook of Lucian's arm, her head on his shoulder while she stroked the hard planes and angles of his chest. Lost in thought and the quiet aftermath of their tumultuous lovemaking, neither one of them had spoken.

For the first time since they'd tumbled into the trailer, Raina glanced around the small bedroom. It was tidy but sparse, with a built-in nightstand on one side of the king-size bed and a small, dark pine dresser on the other side with a stack of books and a baseball sitting on top. A navy-blue valance trimmed the narrow windows and multicolored throw rugs covered pale-blue carpeting. Through the doorway, into the living section of the trailer, past a narrow kitchen and eating area, was a small dark-blue couch and more built-in cupboards. She assumed the bathroom was the closed door next to the bedroom.

A sharp contrast to the spectacular house he was building, but cozy. Very cozy, she thought, and burrowed into the warmth of his arm.

He broke the silence first.

"Was that how it was before?" His voice was rough, edged with amazement.

After she'd told Lucian about Emma, Raina had known that questions about that first night would eventually come up. She'd dreaded having this discussion. Until now. Now it simply seemed natural.

She rose on her elbow, cradled her head in her hand while she made circles on his chest with her fingertips. "Before?"

"Don't be coy, sweetheart." He frowned at her, but there was amusement in his eyes. "You know exactly what I mean."

"Yes." The dark sprinkling of hair of his chest tickled her fingers. "That's exactly how it was."

He lifted both brows and blew out a breath. "Wow."

"Yeah." She smiled, would have purred if she were a cat. "Wow."

"Raina." His hand covered hers. "I'm sorry I wasn't there. When you woke up, I mean. I don't know why I left like I did, I may never know, but I'm sure I would have come back. The note proves that."

"It happened, Lucian," she said with a sigh. "We can't change it. Even if I could, I wouldn't. Every time I look at Emma, I'm so thankful for what that night gave me. Speaking of—" she sat and looked for a phone "—I need to call Melanie."

He reached beside the bed and came up with a cell phone that he'd been charging in the wall socket. He dialed for her, then handed her the phone. Melanie answered on the first ring.

"Mel, I'm so sorry," Raina said into the phone, tried not to notice that Lucian's hand had slipped back under the covers. "We got caught out in the open in the storm." She sucked in a breath when he found the curve of her breast. "*Yes*, I mean, yes, of course, we're fine. I was worried about Emma. Did the thunder wake her? Oh, good, I'm so glad."

He nipped at her neck, nibbled on her earlobe, all while his hand caressed and kneaded. Raina struggled to find her voice. "Oh, they are? Well, we…should be there…soon." She bit back a moan when his hand moved lower. "Very soon, I'm sure."

The texture of his rough hand sliding over her belly sent shivers of intense pleasure racing through her. She hadn't even hung up the phone before he slipped into her, stroking her gently…surely. Sparks danced and shimmered over her skin, and when his mouth blazed hot, wet kisses down her neck and continued south, the sparks ignited into fire.

"What did Melanie say?" he murmured.

"She—" Words bounced in her brain and she fought to grab them. "Emma's fine. Sydney and—" she gripped a handful of the soft comforter when his mouth closed over her hardened nipple "—Abby came over to visit for a while. Melanie said—" she arched upward as his hand and mouth seemed to move with the same rhythm "—to take our time."

He moved over her suddenly, a dark, primal look in his eyes as he pulled her underneath him and slid his hands up her thighs. "Is that what you want to do?" he asked roughly. "Take our time?"

"No," she gasped, and reached for him.

And there it was again. The fury. The raw, naked need. It moved through them like a tornado, uncontrollable and wild, as spectacular as it was thrilling.

They let it take them until, breathless and shattered, they collapsed in each other's arms.

"So this is where you live."

"Most of the time." Lucian pulled a jar of instant coffee from the cupboard beside his small stove and set it on the counter, then reached into a drawer for a spoon. Raina sat at the kitchen table behind him, her legs tucked under her. He'd put on dry clothes and given her a white button-down shirt of his to wear, but she'd had to struggle back into her damp jeans. At least the storm had moved on, and the mid-afternoon sun peeked through the parting clouds.

"When I'm working on a big construction project

I sleep in the trailer on the site," he said. "But this is my home base."

"Quite a place."

He glanced over his shoulder to see if there was any sarcasm in her eyes, but there wasn't. She seemed genuinely interested and charmed by his humble abode. Her hair had dried and now fell in a tumbled mass of dark curls around her shoulders. At the sight of her sitting here, wearing his shirt, with her hair mussed and lips still swollen and rosy from his kisses, he felt something hitch in his chest.

"I get by." At the insistent beep of the microwave, he opened the door, pulled out two steaming mugs and dumped two spoonfuls of coffee in each one.

"Microwave, TV, electricity and plumbing," she said with a smile. "I'd say you get by just fine."

He set the mugs on the table and slid into the booth across from her. Damn, but she was beautiful, he thought, felt his gut tighten at the sight of her blowing on her coffee. Once again he cursed the fact that he couldn't remember the night they'd spent together. His mind and his body still reeled from their short afternoon of lovemaking, and he couldn't help but wonder what an entire night had been like. What it would *be* like.

He wanted to know. One afternoon with this woman wasn't enough.

He wanted more.

As if she read his thoughts, their eyes met. Her smile slowly faded and she looked down at her cup.

He reached for her hand and pulled it toward him. Lightly he traced her knuckles with his thumb, marveled at how soft her skin felt.

"Raina, I think we should get married."

"Why, Lucian?" she asked quietly. "Because we're good in bed together?"

"No." His hand tightened on hers, then he relaxed. "But that doesn't hurt, you know."

She pulled her hand away. "It's no reason to get married."

"Emma's a good reason."

"We've covered that ground already," she said evenly. "I told you that I won't ever keep Emma from you. She'll know who her father is. You can see her whenever you like."

"In New York?" He bit back the crude word that was on the tip of his tongue. "On holidays and vacations? A weekend here and there when it suits you? I want more than that, dammit."

"What are you saying? That you want joint custody?" The look in her eyes turned icy blue. "You think our daughter should live here? In this trailer, with God knows how many women coming through that revolving door of your bedroom?"

He went still at her comment, felt the anger ripple through him. He struggled to gain control, then slowly, carefully said, "I have never brought a woman here before. And I most certainly never would while my daughter was under the same roof. And since you brought up the subject, what about you? How do I know who'll be sleeping in your bed while my daughter's in the next room?"

Just the thought of it turned his anger white-hot, made his gut tighten. What would happen once she was back in New York?

He didn't want to think about it, dammit. He

couldn't. Not without yelling or slamming his fist into a wall.

"I deserve that." She closed her eyes, sighed heavily. "But I have to ask, Lucian. If Emma is going to come here for visits, especially when she comes without me, I have to know."

He took in a slow breath, waited a moment for the anger to dissipate. "I wasn't suggesting joint custody," he said evenly. "I don't believe in shuffling a kid back and forth between households. As much as I'd want to be with her, I wouldn't do that to her."

"I know you wouldn't." Her shoulders relaxed a bit. "I've watched you these past few days. You're terrific with her. She already adores you."

"Then marry me and let me give her my name." He leaned forward. "It could be temporary. For a year or two. When she's old enough to understand, she'll at least think that we cared enough about her to give it a try."

"And you think a divorce will make her feel better that her parents aren't together?" She shook her head. "Lucian, I married once for the wrong reasons. I can't ever do that again."

"And what if you do decide to get married again?" The idea made his blood turn hot. "What then? What rights will I have?"

"Nothing would change between you and Emma if I get married. She'll always be your daughter."

"See that you remember that. Because I'm always going to be in her life, Raina. Always. And that means I'll be in your life, too. Accept it."

"You might be in my life, Lucian," she said tightly. "But that doesn't mean you'll be in my bed every time you get the itch. That *you* had better accept. If you want a formal agreement between us, one of us can contact a lawyer to handle the paperwork.''

''I don't want a damn lawyer.'' It was all he could do not to shake her. ''I want to see Emma when *I* want. Not when some damn piece of paper says.''

''All right.'' She drew in a slow breath. ''You can come to New York as often as you want, and I'll come to Bloomfield at least every other month. As she gets older, we'll increase the length of time she can stay here. When she starts school, we'll discuss vacations and holidays. Now I have to get back.'' She slid out of the booth and pulled her shoes on. ''I've already been gone too long, and Emma will be up from her nap by now.''

Damn stubborn woman, he thought as he followed her out of the trailer. By the rigid set of her back and shoulders, he knew there'd be no more discussion for now. Which was probably for the best, since he also knew he would have started yelling if they had continued.

She climbed into the truck before he could help her, which only aggravated him all the more. He kept his hands tightly on the wheel and his jaw clenched on the ride home. She kept her arms folded and her eyes straight ahead. He snapped a Nirvana tape into the dash player and turned it up, effectively blocking out any chance of conversation.

When he parked in front of Gabe's house, she unhooked her seat belt and slid out of the truck. She was already on the front porch by the time he'd shut off the engine and caught up with her. Dammit, they hadn't even talked about money or medical insurance or schooling. He wasn't about to let all this drop, just because *she* didn't want to talk about it.

He grabbed her hand as she opened the front door. "Look, Raina, you and I need to—"

They both froze at the sight of Abby standing in front of them with Emma in her arms and a worried look on her face.

"What's wrong?" both he and Raina asked at the same time.

"It's Melanie," she said, her voice tight. "Gabe just took her to the hospital. She started bleeding."

Nine

Raina had always hated hospitals. The smell of antiseptic, the hushed tones, the stark, dimly lit halls and rooms. She'd only been eighteen the two weeks she'd spent at The City of Hope in Los Angeles, watching and waiting while her mother slowly gave in to the cancer. She'd tried to locate her father, but he'd moved away her freshman year of high school and she'd had no idea where he'd gone. She still had no idea. After she'd buried her mother, she'd gone off to college on a scholarship and modeled part-time and she'd never looked back.

Except for Melanie. Until Emma, Melanie had been her only family. And now Melanie was in the hospital.

Trembling with the cold fear that wracked her body, Raina sat stiffly on the waiting room chair, her eyes squeezed shut. The cold was suddenly replaced by a warm, strong arm that gently pulled her close.

"Raina—" she heard Lucian say her name "—she's going to be fine. They're both fine."

Still numb, she glanced up, turned toward him as she gripped the front of his denim jacket. "Melanie? And the baby, too?"

"Melanie's still groggy from the cesarean, but everything went well. And based on the way my new niece is hollering, I'd say she's more than fine."

"Oh, thank God, thank God." She couldn't stop the tears of relief. "A girl. A little girl. Are you sure she's all right?"

"All the tests came out perfect." He grinned at her. "If you have to worry about anyone, worry about Gabe. He looks like hell."

She laughed, let herself enjoy the comfort of his arms. "What happened?"

He shook his head. "Gabe's still a little dazed, but from what I could gather, it's something called an abruption. It could have been serious, but in her case, because it wasn't severe and he got her to the hospital so quickly, they were able to do a C-section before it became critical."

"I was so scared." She shuddered, pressed her face into his chest. "So incredibly scared."

"It's all right now, baby," he murmured and pulled her closer. "Everyone's fine. You have to come see my new niece. She's tiny and pink and beautiful. They named her Kayla."

"Kayla." She smiled, knew that Melanie and Gabe had already picked that name if they'd had a girl, and

Kyle if they'd had a boy. "We have to call Abby and Sydney. They must be worried sick."

"Callan already took care of that." He stroked her hair away from her face. "Stop worrying."

Sydney had gone to pick Kevin up from school and bring him back to the house and Abby had stayed with Emma. Cara and Ian were on their way from Philadelphia and Reese and Callan had shown up a few minutes ago, then gone to check on Gabe.

It amazed Raina how quickly everyone had pulled together for Melanie. Without question, there wasn't one Sinclair who wouldn't go the distance for a family member. Emma would be a part of that, Raina realized with a swell of joy. No matter what happened, every Sinclair would be there for Lucian's daughter. The bond between them all was as strong as it was fierce. Emma would always be loved unconditionally, and she would always be protected because she was a Sinclair.

A Sinclair.

In a heartbeat it became as sharp and as clear as cut crystal. She knew what she had to do. She couldn't think about herself anymore. What she wanted or needed didn't matter. Raina knew she had to think of Emma.

She straightened, drew in a deep breath as she looked into eyes that made her think of black emeralds.

"Lucian—" she surprised herself at how strong her voice sounded "—if you still want to get married, my answer is yes."

* * *

"Lucian, I swear, you clench that jaw of yours any tighter, you're gonna break a tooth."

Arms folded high on his chest, Lucian frowned darkly at Reese. "If you don't wipe that smirk off your face, bro, I'm gonna break one of *your* teeth."

"Sounds like someone's a little testy today." Callan pushed away from the porch railing and moved beside Reese. It was a beautiful spring afternoon. Clear, blue sky. Warm. The scent of roses drifted in the air.

"'Course, it being your wedding day," Reese said, "we'll forgive you."

Lucian had known it was coming, of course. The jokes and wisecracks. But that didn't mean he had to like it. Lord knew, he'd thrown more than a few well-placed digs at each of his brothers on their wedding day.

Payback was hell.

Pulling at the gray silk tie choking his neck, he took a threatening step toward his brothers. "Yeah, well, I've got your forgive—"

"Now, now, boys," Ian reprimanded in a school-teacher tone as he stepped from the house onto the front porch. "Your 'plays well with others' column is about to get a very low mark."

"Just what I need," Lucian said dryly. "Larry, Moe and Curly. What the hell is taking so long in there? We were supposed to start ten minutes ago."

"Five minutes ago, actually." Grinning, Ian slapped a hand on the groom's shoulder. "But, after catching a glimpse of your bride, I understand your impatience."

His bride.

Lucian felt his throat turn to dust; his chest squeezed the air out of his lungs. Dear Lord, he was actually getting *married*.

He wanted to. More than anything, he wanted Emma to legally have his name. Wanted her to know that she was completely accepted, not only by him, but by all the Sinclairs.

But was Emma the only one he truly wanted to have his name? he wondered.

He knew why Raina had changed her mind about marrying him four days ago and why she had rescheduled her flight back to New York. The scare with Melanie and little Kayla had sent Raina's emotions into an upheaval. He'd felt it, too. He realized at that moment that being a parent, being responsible for another life, forced a person to face their own mortality. That realization had staggered him. Humbled him.

Empowered him.

He knew there was nothing he couldn't do, nothing he wouldn't do for his child.

Tomorrow Raina was taking Emma and going back to New York. They'd agreed he could visit anytime he wanted, and she'd assured him that she would come to Bloomfield as often as her business allowed.

It wasn't enough. It wasn't even close to being enough. But for now, at least, he knew it would have to do.

He blinked. The Three Stooges were staring at him, and he realized he'd been completely lost in his thoughts. ''What?'' he snapped, annoyed at the amusement on their faces.

"They just gave us the sign." Ian swept a hand toward the front door. "After you."

"Raina, for heaven's sake, stop fidgeting," Melanie said from the cushioned easy chair in her and Gabe's bedroom. Nestled in her mother's arms, baby Kayla slept peacefully in her pink romper. "And don't bite that fingernail, either. You'll mess up your lipstick and your nail polish."

"I'm not fidgeting." Raina jerked her finger away from her mouth and clasped her hands tightly in front of her. "I'm just anxious to get this over with, that's all."

"Spoken like a true bride. Here we go now." Sydney pulled up the zipper of the cream silk sheath dress Raina had on, then held up the matching short jacket. "This is perfect."

Raina slipped her arms into the jacket and smoothed the front. It was the same dress she'd worn at Emma's christening, and she'd had Teresa ship it to her overnight from New York. It had only been delivered three hours ago, which had put all the other women in near heart failure. Especially when Raina had pulled out a black dress she'd brought with her and told them she'd wear that instead. She'd been teasing—sort of—but even Raina had to admit she'd been relieved when the delivery man rang the doorbell.

"Oh, Raina, you look beautiful." Abby shifted Emma from one arm to the other. "Doesn't your mommy look pretty, sweetheart?"

Emma cooed approvingly, and all the women laughed.

Warmed by the compliment, and the other
women's enthusiasm, Raina couldn't help but smile,
too. In spite of the fact that it wasn't a real wedding
or a real marriage, she'd wanted to look nice. Wanted
to remember this as a special day.

All heads turned at the quiet knock at the door, and
Cara slipped in, her cheeks flushed with excitement.

"The minister just got here," Cara said, then
gasped. "Oh, Raina, you look stunning."

"I can't wait until Lucian sees her." Sydney
straightened Raina's collar. "That man's jaw is going
to hit the ground."

Just the mention of his name had her stomach doing backflips. Sudden overwhelming panic gripped
her.

She hadn't wanted all this fuss. A justice of the
peace would have been fine. But once word had
spread in the family that Lucian was getting married,
there'd been no stopping the Sinclair women. Lucian
had gone along with it, and even Melanie, her best
friend, had been a part of the conspiracy. So now
there were twenty or so guests downstairs, people she
didn't know. Friends and co-workers of Lucian's. A
minister. All waiting for a wedding.

All waiting for her.

She couldn't breathe.

"Uh-oh." Sydney guided her toward the bed and
eased her on to the edge. "Just put your head down,
honey, and take slow, easy breaths."

"I...I'm sorry," she gasped between breaths.
"This is...so unfair to you all. You shouldn't...have
gone to...so much trouble. It's not...we're not—"

She dropped her face in her hands. She couldn't pretend, couldn't continue with this farce.

"We're only getting married for Emma," she whispered hoarsely and lifted her head in anguish. "Lucian and I don't love each other like all of you love your husbands."

The women all exchanged a knowing look, then smiled with patient understanding.

Cara took Raina's hand and squeezed. "It's perfectly normal to be nervous on your wedding day. I broke out in hives the morning of mine."

"But we don't love each other," Raina insisted. "Melanie knows it's true. You've all been so wonderful to me, I don't want to lie to you. We aren't going to live together, and in a year or two we're going to get divorced."

Sydney sat beside her and slipped an arm around her. "Well then, I guess we better enjoy the time we're sisters-in-law, shouldn't we?"

Emma babbled happily when Abby sat down on the bed next to Raina and slipped an arm around her, too. At the unexpected display of affection, Raina couldn't stop the tears.

"Hey, what about me?" Melanie complained. "I'm stuck over here."

Laughing, the women hurried over to Melanie and, careful not to disturb the sleeping baby, they all gently hugged.

"Tissue," Abby managed on a sob and reached for the box sitting on the dresser.

A knock at the door had them all turning.

"Hey," Gabe called from the hallway. "Lucian's

just about worn a hole in the rug downstairs. You ladies ready?''

Eyes wide, Raina shook her head.

"One more minute," Sydney called back and they all scrambled, pulling on high heels and dabbing at makeup.

"Something old." Melanie reached in her pocket and pulled out an antique tortoiseshell hair clip.

"Something new." Abby pressed a white lace handkerchief in Raina's hand.

"Something borrowed." Sydney clasped a beautiful pearl choker around Raina's neck.

"Something blue." Smiling, Cara swung a blue-and-white lace garter around her finger and before Raina could refuse, it was already on her leg.

Sydney moved to the door and opened it. Gabe stood on the other side with Kevin, who pulled at the collar of the starched white shirt under his suit.

Gabe's eyes went to his wife first, softened at the sight of her with their baby, then he glanced at Raina and winked.

Her eyes darted frantically around the room.

"Quick, close the window before she jumps out," Melanie teased.

Laughing, Gabe scooped up his wife and child in his arms. It would be at least two weeks, he'd flatly informed her when he'd brought her home from the hospital, before she would be walking up or down any stairs. "Ready?"

No!

Abby and Sydney flanked her and led her to the top of the stairs. At the sound of the music, Raina tried to take a step back, but they gently held her in place. Sydney pressed a bouquet of white roses into her hands and kissed her cheek.

At the sound of the wedding march, she swallowed hard, then slowly, step by step, made her way down the stairs on legs that felt like wood.

And then there were no more steps.

Her eyes met his as she walked into the living room, between the white folding chairs and down the makeshift aisle. Toward him. She no longer heard the music, no longer saw the people surrounding her.

There was only Lucian.

His suit was deep charcoal, his silk tie dark gray against a soft gray shirt. She remembered the first time she'd laid eyes on him, the way her knees had turned to water and her insides to warm taffy. It was no different now, and she had to force herself to concentrate, to put one foot in front of the other and hold her head straight, or she'd make a fool of herself for certain.

More of a fool than she already had, anyway.

He watched her with those sharp, piercing, green eyes of his, took in every detail from head to toe, then back up again. A slow masculine perusal that made her skin heat up and her heart pound harder and faster than it already was.

Somehow she managed to say the words, to slip a band on his finger and accept the ring he'd slipped on hers. To close her eyes and press her lips to his in response to the customary "you may kiss the bride."

And she let herself pretend, for just those few minutes, that it wasn't smoke and mirrors.

"Where in the world did all these people come from?" Beer in hand, Lucian stood in the shadow of a large spruce. Beside him, Gabe leaned against the thick trunk of his backyard tree. "I don't remember inviting Mabel and Henry Binderby."

In fact, he didn't remember inviting at least half of the people who'd drifted in, slowly but surely, throughout the course of the evening. There'd been so many bodies in the house at one point, they'd all finally dragged a few tables and chairs outside and spilled into the backyard. Music pounded from Gabe's stereo system, and Sydney had candles and tablecloths sent over from her restaurant, along with additional trays of pasta primavera, salad and rolls. Reese called in for reinforcements from his tavern, and a truck with a fresh keg of beer and a case of champagne had shown up an hour ago.

So much for the small wedding his family had insisted on.

"People just want to be here for this great historical event," Gabe said. "Lucian Sinclair's wedding will keep the gossip lines burning up for weeks. I've already heard four different versions of how and where you proposed, not to mention the romantic honeymoon you're taking in St. Thomas. Hey, isn't that Sally Lyn Wetters with Laura Greenley?"

Lucian choked on the beer he'd been about to swallow. Good Lord, it was one thing to have regular townspeople here, but *girlfriends?* he thought in dismay. Well, ex-girlfriends, anyway.

Terrific. Sally Lyn had spotted him and was already headed his way. Her lips were as bright red as her dress, and any other time he would have appreciated the pretty blonde.

But the only woman on his mind at this moment was Raina.

From the moment she'd walked down that aisle toward him, looking like the heavens had opened up and she was his special gift, every other woman he'd ever known no longer existed. Just Raina. With her smoky-blue eyes fixed on his, her dark, glorious hair swept up off her long neck, her rosy lips curved softly in a smile, she was everything a man could have ever dreamed of wanting. She absolutely dazzled him.

He searched her out now, found her standing on the back porch, laughing with Rafe Barclay, Bloomfield's sheriff. Jealousy, as unwelcome as it was unfamiliar, speared through him. Rafe was single and good-looking—so the women told him—and he wasn't shy or reserved when it came to the female gender.

Rafe was also his friend; they'd gone all the way through school together. Went fishing at the lake every few weeks and played poker on Saturday nights if they weren't out on a date. There'd been lots of playful competition between them, but Lucian had never once been jealous.

Not until now, at least.

"Yoo-hoo, Lucian." Sally Lyn waved as she made her way closer. "Why are you hiding over here?"

Lucian tried not to think about what Rafe had said to make Raina laugh or her eyes sparkle the way they did. Instead he forced a smile and thought about how relieved he was that he'd never slept with Sally Lyn. Otherwise, this would be way too awkward.

"Gabe," Lucian whispered under his breath. "So

help me, if you value your life, don't you dare leave me alone.''

Chuckling, Gabe pushed away from the tree, then lifted his beer bottle in a silent toast as he walked off.

He'd kill him later, Lucian thought, then decided that since he had a wife and two kids, he'd simply maim him.

"Congratulations, Lucian," Sally Lyn purred as she sidled up next to him and kissed him square on the mouth. "I just want to wish you and your new wife the best."

"Thanks." He shifted uncomfortably, not sure what to say.

"I must say, though." She pursed her lips into a perfect pout. "I am, well, surprised."

"Life's a surprise, isn't it?" His gaze went back to Raina, narrowed when both she and Rafe were gone. "You never know what's going to happen."

"That is so true." She giggled and ran a finger down his suit lapel. "Especially with you, Lucian. You always were so impulsive."

"Isn't he, though?"

Lucian turned at the sound of Raina's voice. He'd been so busy looking for her with Rafe, he hadn't seen her skirt the edge of the crowd and come up from the side. Sally Lyn dropped her hand away and stepped back.

"Raina," he said, more than a little uncomfortable. "This is Sally Lyn Wetters. Sally Lyn, Raina."

Sally Lyn held out her hand. "Lucian and I are old...friends," she said with just enough emphasis on the word *friends* to raise one of Raina's brows.

"How nice for you."

Four little words spoken with such cool, bored so-phistication that Sally Lyn had no response.

"Yes, well—" Sally Lyn cleared her throat "—it was nice to meet you."

Raina nodded, smiled, but said nothing.

"Bye, Lucian." Sally Lyn glanced at him, then sighed and walked away.

"Raina—"

"They're going to cut the cake in a few minutes," she said evenly. "Since your family's gone to all this trouble, we should make an appearance."

"Raina—"

"You also might want to wipe Sally Lyn's lipstick from your mouth." She handed him a clean tissue from the pocket of her silk jacket. "It's not even close to my color."

Frowning, he took the tissue and wiped the lipstick from his mouth and stared at the red stain. What the hell was he feeling so guilty for? He hadn't done a damn thing.

"We used to date," he said tightly. "That's it. I never even slept with the woman."

"Did I ask?" Her gaze held his. "We might be married, but we both know it's for Emma. For how-ever long we decide to stay married, I won't question what you do or with whom. In return, I expect the same courtesy."

A muscle jumped at the corner of his eye. He didn't like the direction of this conversation one little bit. And he definitely didn't like the implication that she might be dating or sleeping with someone else. Es-pecially while she was married to him.

He took hold of her arm and pulled her close to him. "What the hell are you trying to say?"

"I thought I was pretty clear," she said calmly, though her breathing had deepened. "I'm not expecting you to be celibate, Lucian, though for appearances, you should at least be discreet."

"Well, how very generous of you." His hand tightened on her arm. "And I suppose you'll be 'discreet' as well."

"I can control myself."

"Is that so?" A fury built inside him at the very thought of her with someone else, a fury mixed with desire from wanting her so badly he thought he might go mad if he didn't have her. He dipped his head, brought his lips within a finger's width of hers. To his satisfaction, her lips parted. "Is that what you were doing in my bed a few days ago, sweetheart, controlling yourself?"

It took a moment for his words to register, then her shoulders went rigid. She glanced quickly away, then closed her eyes and sighed.

"I'm sorry, Lucian," she said quietly. "I don't want us to argue the last night I'm here. It's just been a long day and I'm a little out of sorts."

He nodded, then relaxed his hold on her. "I think it's safe to say it's been a long day for both of us."

"I have a ten-o'clock flight in the morning," she said awkwardly. "I can ask Gabe to take me and Emma to the airport, if you'd rather."

He wanted to shake her, tell her she was his *wife* and she damn well wasn't going anywhere. But he knew in the long run it would only make things worse. She would still leave and his pride would have holes from her high heels as she walked away.

"I'll take you," he said tightly.

She stepped away from him and smiled, though it never reached her eyes. "Shall we go cut the cake now?"

"Fine."

Frustrated, he waited a moment to calm down before he followed her. He'd cut the cake, he thought, gritting his teeth. A great big piece. And he'd smash every little crumb in her pretty little face.

Ten

"**J**anice, have Brandy take a tuck in that strap. Lidia, you're supposed to wear the blue push-up, not the black strapless and Jill, for heaven's sake, put some adhesive on under that bra."

Struggling to remain calm in the midst of chaos, Raina sat cross-legged on the floor of the backstage dressing area and snipped off a loose thread on the side seam of a silver satin nightgown. Deidre, the red-headed model wearing the nightgown, did a slow 360-degree turn while Raina inspected the hem.

"Twenty minutes." Annelise, Raina's assistant, hurried by, her arms filled with a cloud of white tulle.

The knot in Raina's stomach twisted tighter.

"Raina, ple-ease." Aurel, a blond model from the Bronx, stormed over, thrust her hands on her slender hips and stuck her lower lip out. "Please let me wear the spiked leather choker with the black camisole."

"Aurie," Raina said patiently after she'd counted to three. "We're not doing a shoot for *Babes on Bikes*. Now spit out your gum and stand up straight."

The woman might be gorgeous and knew how to work a crowd, Raina thought with a sigh, but she had no sense of fashion, and you could almost hear the echo if you spoke too close to her ear.

"Fifteen minutes." Annelise rushed by again, this time clutching a plush teddy bear that one of the sleepwear models would be carrying on her walk down the runway.

Breathe, Raina told herself. Slow, easy, breaths...
Slow, easy, breaths...

The same exact words that Sydney had used the day that Raina Sarbanes had become Mrs. Lucian Sinclair. The day her life had completely turned upside down and inside out.

That day seemed so long ago now, a lifetime, though it had actually only been eight days. Seven days since Lucian had driven her and Emma to the airport. They'd barely spoken more than a few polite words on the ride there, and the tension between them had been stretched taut as piano wire. He'd kissed and hugged Emma, and Raina had seen the frustration in his narrowed eyes when he'd handed their daughter back, but he'd said nothing. He hadn't touched her. He'd just nodded and given her a tight goodbye.

He hadn't called once.

Not that she'd been home very much since she and Emma had gotten back to New York. She'd been busy every minute getting ready for the show. Except for today, Raina had brought Emma and her nanny to the office with her every day this past week, so there'd been no one home. But she had a machine. He could have left a message if he'd called.

Or she could have called him.

She'd picked up the phone at least once a day for the past six days with the intention of calling him. Then hung up. Picked it up again.

Hung up again.

Why was it so damn hard to say she was sorry?

Blowing a strand of hair out of her eyes, she snipped another loose thread from the hem of the nightgown. She knew she'd apologized at the reception, but she needed to say it again. Maybe she *had* overreacted just a little to that pretty blonde hanging on him. But when she'd seen that, that *hussy* kiss Lucian right on the mouth and hang herself on him like a tacky red painting on a wall, well, for crying out loud, what was she supposed to feel? She'd wanted to scratch the woman's eyes out.

She still wanted to scratch the woman's eyes out.

After the reception, after everyone had finally left and everything was cleaned up, she knew he'd wanted her to invite him into the bedroom. But she hadn't. She'd been too keyed-up from the day. If they had slept in the same room, they would have made love.

She had felt too vulnerable to let him that close, was afraid she would lose the last thread of control and tell him that she loved him. That she didn't want to go. That she wanted a *real* marriage.

So he'd slept on the couch and she'd slept in that big four-poster bed, alone, letting the tears fall.

"Raina, did you want the three-inch black heels with the black embroidered bra or the satin under-wire?"

Raina glanced up at the sound of her assistant's question and blinked. "What?"

Annelise pushed her big, black horn-rimmed glasses up her nose, then held up two different bras. "Did you want the three-inch black heels with the—"

When Annelise stopped midsentence, Raina finished for her. "The three-inch for the satin underwire. Four-inch black T-strap for the embroidered."

When Annelise didn't respond or move away, Raina suddenly realized that not only had her assistant gone quiet, so had the entire room, which was unheard of in a room full of twenty women before a show.

Frowning, Raina looked up, noticed that every woman in the place was looking behind her.

She turned.

Oh, dear Lord.

Slow, deep breaths...

Lucian stood two feet away, looking a little flustered, but so incredibly, wonderfully handsome in a hunter-green dress shirt and black dress jeans and boots, that every woman in the place had to be licking her lips.

She knew she was.

"Lucian," she gasped, then stood up so quickly that he had to reach out and steady herself or she would have fallen over.

"Hey, handsome," one of the models called out. "Can you come over here and zip me up?"

To his credit Lucian did not respond. Carefully he kept his attention focused on Raina. "I'm sorry, I know this is bad timing. I was just going to sit out front, but when I told the hostess who I was, she ushered me back here.''

''Who are you, sweet-cheeks?'' Aurel asked and moved in like a cat on the prowl. A few of the other models had also moved in, circling like a pack of she-wolves.

''Don't you know, sugar?'' someone said with a fake Southern accent. ''He's my hero.''

The remark triggered a flurry of alternative suggestions regarding who the handsome stranger was, until Raina finally said quite loudly, ''He's my husband.''

Instant silence.

Well, at least everyone was staring at *her* now, Raina thought, instead of Lucian. Even her assistant's eyes were huge behind her glasses. Since Raina had neglected to mention the little fact that she'd gotten married while she was in Bloomfield, she could only imagine the shock she'd just given everyone. It might have been funny if it wasn't so distressing.

''Lucian, what are you doing here?'' she said as calmly as she could possibly manage. Her heart hammered furiously against her ribs.

''You said I could visit whenever I wanted.'' He glanced sideways at the scantily clad models who'd leaned in close to listen, then quickly looked back at Raina and swallowed hard. ''I, ah, forgot this was a lingerie show.''

''So you just show up?'' She was torn between throwing her arms around him and kissing him or booting him out. How could he just show up here like this? Looking so wonderful, so *magnificent*.

She knew what every woman in the room was

thinking because she was thinking exactly the same thing.

Hubba-hubba.

"I went to your apartment," he said. "The nanny wouldn't let me in, but she told me I could find you here."

"For heaven's sake, Lucian, I can't talk to you now. I've got a show in—" she glanced at her watch "—oh, my God! Three minutes! Everyone, get in place, get ready. Jamie, you're first, straighten that strap and put some more lip gloss on. Aurel, take that choker off right this minute. Annelise, see that my— that Mr. Sinclair is escorted out front, please."

Everyone scurried and shifted to work mode, though Raina couldn't help but notice the longing glances that followed Lucian out of the room. Lord knew that her own gaze lingered on those broad shoulders longer than she had intended.

The sound of the master of ceremonies welcoming everyone jolted Raina back to the show. The loud, heavy beat of ZZ Top's "She's Got Legs" signaled the start.

The first model sashayed out, and for the next thirty minutes, Raina somehow managed to keep her mind off Lucian Sinclair and on her work.

Champagne flowed freely in the twenty-first-floor executive suite of the Hilton Hotel and Towers. A tuxedo-clad waiter carried a silver tray of miniature bruschetta and goose pâté on crackers for the crowd. Several bodies swayed to a musical mix of jazz, latin and rock tunes, while others huddled around the bar, arguing fashion trends: who was in and who was out.

At the moment Raina's new line of lingerie called "Whisper," was definitely in.

Lucian stood next to a fake palm in the corner, content to simply watch as Raina, dressed in a simple, black silk evening dress, mingled with her guests, graciously and modestly accepting the exuberant praise from the critics, buyers and designers she'd invited to the party.

Three weeks ago he'd have thought himself the luckiest man on earth. He'd had a front row seat at a lingerie fashion show and was currently surrounded by tall, gorgeous women. Any other red-blooded male would have thought he'd died and gone to heaven.

But he wasn't any other man, and it wasn't three weeks ago. Three weeks ago his life had changed, and this past week, without Emma, without Raina, had been hell. Everything about his life now, about himself, felt different.

At this moment there was only one tall, gorgeous woman he wanted to be with.

His wife.

He wanted everyone else gone.

Especially Aurel, he thought with a silent sigh, the blond, gum-popping model who'd been talking to him for the past five minutes about the date she'd had on some TV show called *Blind Date*.

"So I said to the guy, I said, like, who do you think you are, like, Mel Gibson? And he says, who do you think *you* are, like, Julia Roberts? Can you imagine, comparing *me* to Julia Roberts, that was just way cool and then he said..."

He nodded, offered an occasional "hmm," or "really?" while Aurel continued with a minute-by-minute description of her television debut, but he kept his gaze on Raina, who was shaking the hand of a dark-haired man wearing a black Armani suit. From the few words Lucian managed to hear, he was certain the man was Italian.

When the man leaned forward and whispered something in Raina's ear, Lucian narrowed his eyes. She smiled and her brow lifted in interest as the man continued to speak softly to her, then with a sigh, she looked back at the Italian and reluctantly shook her head.

Bastard. Lucian gritted his teeth. The guy was trying to hit on Raina. And right under her own husband's nose, no less. He'd like to stuff the guy's fancy gold cuff links down his throat and pull them out his—

"Hey, sugar." A tall, buxom, raven-haired model, "Kimmie who could shimmy"—so the announcer had said as the woman had sauntered down the walkway—suddenly appeared with two glasses of champagne and moved in close. "Looks like you need something to fill those big hands of yours."

With his back against the wall, Lucian had no place to go. He smiled politely and accepted the glass of champagne she offered, but made no attempt to accept anything else she might be suggesting. While Aurel continued with her detailed account of her evening out on the town with some guy named Steve, Lucian watched Raina take the Italian's arm and lead him over to another group of people.

Dammit. How long did these things last anyway?

He still didn't know what had possessed him to jump on a plane this morning and come here without

so much as a phone call. One minute he'd been framing the tub for the master bath, pounding away while
he listened to Led Zeppelin, the next minute he was
packing a bag and heading for the airport.

Not that he hadn't thought about coming here every
minute of every day for the past week. But thinking
about doing something and actually doing it were two
entirely different things.

And yet, here he was, in New York.

And here she was.

Now if only he could get her alone....

Lucian suddenly realized that another woman had
joined his small group, a redhead with big green eyes
who had the looks of a model but not the height.
She'd said something to him, but he had no idea what.
He played it safe by simply smiling and nodding.

"Terrific." The woman pulled a card out of her
pocket. "Just give me your name and number and I'll
call you."

Oops. Damn, what had she said to him? "Ahh,
well, I—"

"Call him for what?" Raina stepped out of the sea
of people and smiled at the woman. "Hello, Phoebe."

Lucian wanted to kiss Raina, not just because she'd
saved him, but because he wanted to kiss her. All he'd
thought about since she'd left after the wedding was
how much he wanted to be with her. To kiss her. To
make love with her.

Since *that* was obviously out of the question at this
moment, he simply feasted his eyes on her, breathed
in the familiar scent of her and took a sip of champagne.

"Hey, Rae." Phoebe smiled back. "Long time no

see. And your friend here just agreed to a photo shoot.
I've got a contract with Calvin Klein he'd be perfect
for.''

Lucian nearly spit out the champagne in his mouth.
Raina raised both brows and looked at him. ''Oh,
really?''

No, not really, he wanted to say, but he could
hardly tell the woman he hadn't listened to a word
she'd said. A *photo* shoot, for crying out loud. No
way in hell he was doing that.

''I appreciate the offer—'' oh, hell, what was her
name? Oh, yeah ''—Phoebe, but I'm afraid I can't,
I'm not—''

''Phoebe.'' Raina cut him off. ''This is my husband, Lucian Sinclair. Lucian, this is Phoebe Knight.
She's a photographer.''

''Husband?'' Surprise widened Phoebe's eyes. She
glanced from Raina to Lucian, then back at Raina.
''It's been longer than I thought, Rae. We definitely
need to do lunch.''

''We will.'' Raina slipped her arm into Lucian's.
''Now if you'll excuse us, I'm just dying to get this
man alone for a minute.''

''Just for a minute?'' Aurel said in her whisky-
toned voice. ''I'd go for at least ten, honey.''

Lucian smiled at the spread of pink on Raina's
cheeks as she pulled him away, was certain he heard
the buxom model say she'd go for an hour.

''Bless you.'' He slipped an arm around Raina's
waist and whispered in her ear. ''You saved me.''

''You have no idea,'' she said with a lift of her
brow. ''Those two would have eaten you alive.''

Which was, of course, exactly what *she* wanted to

do, Raina thought as she dragged Lucian into a bedroom. A Latin beat, something by Marc Anthony pounded through the door she closed behind them.

She couldn't even be annoyed with Aurel or Kimmie. They were simply being who they were, sirens with a cause, which was to make every living, breathing man adore them. They might be beautiful, but she thought she knew Lucian well enough to guess they weren't his type.

Phoebe, on the other hand, *had* concerned her. She was smart, successful, beautiful, and she didn't intersperse every other word with "like" or "whatever."

"Why in the world would you tell Phoebe that you'd do a shoot for her?" she asked, folding her arms.

He scratched at the back of his neck and shifted from one foot to the other. "Well, I didn't exactly. I was just…I was—"

"Oh, never mind." She closed her eyes and sighed. "It's none of my business, anyway."

She'd told him at the reception that she wouldn't ask him any questions if he didn't ask her any. So what's the first thing she did when she finally got him alone? Like a jealous idiot, she'd started asking questions.

Well, if he wanted to do a photo shoot with Phoebe, he could go right ahead. He could do a hundred if he wanted.

If Phoebe wasn't such a good friend, Raina thought she just might rip every pretty red hair out of her gorgeous head.

Suddenly too tired to even stand, she sank on the

edge of the bed. "It's been a long day, Lucian. I don't have the energy to argue with you."

"Good."

She felt the mattress sink as he sat down beside her on the bed. She might be tired, she realized, but she wasn't dead. Her body came alive at his closeness, and it was there once again—that shimmering awareness of him. The familiar, masculine scent that was his alone, the heat rippling from his long, muscular body, the sensuality that radiated like waves off a New York city street in August.

He looked a little tired, she thought, noticed a tinge of red in his eyes. Had he missed her these past few days? she wondered. Or had he simply been angry at her? As much as she wanted to know, she wouldn't, couldn't ask.

"Congratulations on a successful show," he said, breaking the silence between them. "I liked your stuff. Your designs, I mean."

Considering the women who'd modeled the lingerie, she doubted he'd noticed her designs. Still, she appreciated his effort at complimenting her, and she sure as hell wasn't about to let him see that nasty little streak of jealousy she'd already displayed one too many times when it came to women fawning over him.

"Thanks." She thought about all the orders she'd taken, more than she could have ever dreamed. Why didn't it feel as wonderful as she'd always imagined it would? "It's been a good day."

"I hope I didn't ruin anything by surprising you at the show," he said.

She laughed softly, rolled her sore neck. "My girls

were so pumped up from looking at you backstage they came on the runway like fireballs just to impress you. I do believe I heard the word *sizzling* at least a dozen times this evening, referring to both my designs and my husband.''

He glanced away from her, but not before she saw the blush rise up his neck. It amused and thoroughly charmed her that she'd actually embarrassed him.

They sat shoulder to shoulder, thigh to thigh, careful not to make contact. He wore his wedding band, she realized suddenly, and felt her pulse flutter at the sight. Not quite ready to answer questions from the people she worked with, Raina had slipped hers off when she'd come home. She didn't know if Lucian had noticed or if he cared, but she did know that the emotions between them were still raw, still sensitive, and they were both treading carefully on what could prove to be very thin ice.

''I went to see Emma today. Teresa wouldn't let me in.''

''I told her about you. That we'd gotten married.'' There was a tiny piece of lint on Lucian's black jeans and she had to fold her hands together to keep from plucking it off. ''But she's very cautious with people she doesn't know.''

''I showed her my driver's license, my blood donor card and an airline ticket,'' he said dryly. ''She told me Emma was napping and I should go see you, then slammed the door in my face.''

''She's wonderful with Emma.'' Teresa was like a mother to her, a grandmother to Emma, Raina thought. She didn't know what she would ever do without her. "Don't be angry with her for being careful."

"Angry?" He looked at her with surprise. "I was thinking about giving her a raise. It was comforting to know there's someone like her watching over Emma when you aren't there."

She laughed at his unexpected comment, then stared down at her hands and felt her smile fade.

"Lucian," she said his name softly, "why are you here?"

"To see Emma."

Her chest tightened. She knew, of course, that he'd come to see Emma, but she'd be lying if she couldn't admit, even to herself, that she'd hoped, just maybe, he might have come to see her, too. *Stupid, stupid,* she mentally kicked herself.

"She'll be happy to see you." She forced herself to smile again, then pushed up from the bed to rise. "She's asleep for the night now, but you can come over in the—"

He took hold of her arm and eased her back onto the bed. "And I came to see you, too."

Her heart skipped, then raced. She looked up. "To see me?"

"I didn't like the way things came down between us before you left. I thought I...well, I just want you to know that there really wasn't anything between me and Sally Lyn. That—"

"Lucian, please, I'm sorry I said what I did at the reception. I shouldn't have. And you really don't have to tell me anything that—"

He put his finger to her lips. "That we never even slept together, like I already told you. And I sure as hell never had any thoughts of marrying her, like you may have heard.''

"Really?" She hated that she sounded so happy over that fact, but she couldn't help it. ''Because if you did, if you think that you might—''

''Raina, for God's sake.'' He looked at the ceiling. ''Will you just shut up? This is difficult enough.''

Not sure what to say about that, she shut up, looked down at his hand on her arm. The texture of his callused palm on her skin sent shivers through her.

''I didn't want you to leave last week.''

''I live in New York, Lucian.'' *Why didn't you want me to leave?* Was it just Emma? she wanted to know. Or had he missed her, too? ''My work is here.''

''I know, dammit.'' Frustration had him raking a hand through his hair. ''Look, let me hang around for a few days. I need some time with Emma and—''

He paused and she waited, breath held.

''—I promise I won't get in your way.''

Why had she let herself believe that he might want to spend time with her, too? The hope she'd felt swooped down like a kite caught in a downdraft. A wave of exhaustion rolled through her, as profound as it was heavy, and all she wanted to do was go home and crawl into bed.

''I told you that you could visit anytime you wanted,'' she said with a sigh, then eased her arm from his hand and stood. ''Come over in the morning and—''

She stopped suddenly, listened.

''What?''

''Do you hear that?''

He narrowed his eyes. "I don't hear anything."

"Exactly." She marched to the door and opened it.

The suite was empty. Even the waiter had left.

Raina stared in shock at the deserted room, then glanced at the serving cart that had been rolled in front of the door. There was a note taped to a bottle of champagne chilling in an ice bucket beside two flutes of crystal, a bowl of strawberries and a can of whipped cream.

Lucian came up behind her as she snapped up the note and read: "Congratulations to the Bride and Groom! We're sure you can be as wonderfully creative with the strawberries and whipped cream as you are with your designs! Love, Everyone!"

Lucian chuckled.

She turned abruptly, nearly bumped into him and felt the heat start at her neck and work its way upward.

"They, ah, thought we would want to be alone."

"Imagine that." He reached for the whipped cream, squirted a dollop on his finger and looked at it. "Did you know that I have a weakness for whipped cream?"

When he licked the puffy white cloud of cream from his finger, Raina felt her toes curl. Her lips parted as she stared at his mouth. "I...didn't know that."

"You know what else I have a weakness for?" he said quietly, locking his green gaze on her blue one.

She could barely breathe. "Strawberries?"

He shook his head slowly, kept his gaze on hers as he set the can of whipped cream back down. "You."

Eleven

*Y*ou.

That single word thrilled her, raced through her mind and her body like a firestorm. Made her tremble with anticipation.

"If you want me to leave," he said, his gaze still on hers, "tell me now. Right now."

His voice was strained, quiet as the empty room they stood in. The tension stretched between them like a tightrope, a high-wire that she suddenly found herself on, struggling to keep her balance on what was logical and sane.

Did she want him to leave?

He watched her with those hungry green eyes, and she'd never felt so consumed by a look. It frightened and thrilled her at the same time.

Excited her.

Did she want him to leave?

Not in a million years.

"Stay."

When his arms came around her, when he dragged her against him and crushed his mouth to hers, she felt that rope slip from under her. The fall was as endless as it was exhilarating. Adrenaline pumped wildly through her veins, made her temples pound and her heart sing.

Dizzy from the fall, from the desire swirling through her, she clung to him. His kiss was hard and demanding; the taste of whipped cream and champagne on his tongue was heady. He slanted his head, moved his mouth over hers and deepened the kiss.

Pleasure coiled inside her like a living thing, tighter and tighter.

"Lucian," she gasped, dragging her mouth from his. "We should…the bedroom…"

But then his mouth caught hers again, and she couldn't get the words out. Forgot what the words were.

They moved toward the bedroom, a halting, intimate dance of anxious hands and urgent whispers. She kicked off her heels; he unzipped her dress; buttons opened.

She wanted his hands on her everywhere, wanted her hands on him. A molten river of heat poured through her body. Brazenly she slid her hands over his strong bare chest, down his flat belly, then lower, stroking, caressing. Up, down again.

He groaned, pressed his hardness against her while he dragged her dress from her shoulders and shoved the garment down. And then his hands were filled with her aching breasts and it was her turn to groan.

And gasp.

In one swift move, he had her on her back, on the bed underneath him. Her breath came in short ragged gulps of air. He straddled her, kept his intense gaze on hers as he shrugged out of his shirt, then unbuckled his belt. The hiss of a zipper, the thump of a boot on the floor, then another thump.

She watched, in awe, incapable of speech. He had the body of a man who worked hard at his job: thick, muscled arms; large, callused hands; solid, wide chest. Power and strength emanated from him and quite literally took her breath away.

You.

That single word again. Did he truly have a weakness for her? she wanted to know. And was it only for the physical, or could it possibly be more?

Did she dare hope that it could be?

He moved over her, slid his hands up her thighs and stopped when he hit a sliver of black floral lace.

And smiled.

"Sexy," he murmured as he slowly ran one fingertip along the scalloped edge of her panties, from the outside of her leg to the inside.

"They're called—" she sucked in a breath when he reached the juncture of her thighs "—Shameless."

His finger hesitated, then moved back and forth over the soft mound of lace-covered curls. She bit her lip at the jolt of intense pleasure that shot through her. Heat coiled tightly between her legs, throbbing.

His finger slid underneath lace. "I don't remember this one from the show."

"No, I— Next month's. This is…what you would call a—" her heart stuttered when he slipped inside her "—private showing. Dammit, Lucian," she said on a moan. "If you keep talking, I'm going to have to hurt you."

Chuckling, he dipped his head and sent her reeling. She clutched at his shoulders, arching upward on a gasp. His hands gripped her hips, held her steady while he moved over her. The heat built, curled upward, higher and higher, tighter. She begged him to stop in one breath, pleaded with him to continue in the next.

"Lucian, please," she sobbed. "I want you inside me. I need you inside me."

And then he was. Deep inside her. Not just in her body, she thought in a daze, but in her heart and in her soul.

Where he'd always been. Where he would always be.

She met him with every thrust, felt his muscles tighten and coil under her eager hands. The tempo increased until they both were panting, both falling together, then shuddering from the violent force of release….

"I swear to you I didn't come here for that."

Lucian held her close, brushed his lips over the top of her soft hair. They'd both been quiet in the aftermath of their lovemaking, both lost in their own thoughts. He really hadn't meant for that particular thought to be the first thing out of his mouth, but somehow it just popped out.

"You're lousy at pillow talk, Lucian." She turned

her head into his chest and nipped with her teeth. "I was hoping for something more like, 'amazing,' or 'unbelievable.'"

He rolled so he could look down at her. She smiled, a satisfied, content smile, like a cat who'd just polished off a bowl of cream. "Those words would pale," he said, tucking a strand of hair behind her ear.

A pretty shade of pink rushed over her cheeks. Her gaze dropped. "So what are you saying, that you're sorry we just made love?"

"Good grief, no." Looking at her like this, with her hair fanned out on the pillow, her lips still full and rosy from his kisses, her eyes glazed and smoky with desire, made it hard to remember what he'd been trying to say at all. "I've never been sorry about making love with you. I'm only sorry I can't remember that first time. It frustrates the hell out of me."

"Nothing like that...like you..." she said, keeping her eyes averted from his, "had ever happened to me before. It was like we'd been caught in a tornado." Her finger traced a slow circle on his chest. "It's still like that, Lucian," she said softly. "I could play games and deny it, but coy has never been my style. Sex with you is incredible."

Sex? Why did her casual use of the word suddenly annoy him? Was that all they were doing? Having sex?

Or was it more?

He'd never felt anything like this, for any woman. It confused the hell out of him, made him...nervous.

Whatever it was, he knew that he wanted Raina. In bed and out. And not simply because she was the mother of his child or because she was a beautiful woman. But because she was Raina. He'd missed her this past week. Missed her smile, the sound of her laugh, the way her eyes danced when she held Emma and played with her. He'd felt an emptiness he'd never known before.

He'd felt...lonely.

Jeez, that sounded pathetic. Since when had he ever been lonely? He had a big family, nephews, a niece, friends. And Emma. Just the thought of her made his chest tighten. He had it all. Damn, but he was getting sappy. If he wasn't careful, he'd be writing poetry and cutting out little lace hearts.

He shook off his thoughts, turned his attention back to the moment and the woman in his arms. Her fingertips were still moving over his chest, and her touch stirred the heat again, made his heart beat faster and his blood race.

"Raina." He said her name softly. "I have some time, a week or two, before we break ground on our next project. I can get a hotel room close to your place, spend some time with Emma."

And you, he said silently.

Her fingers hesitated, then moved again. "She'd love that."

"Great." Why had he wanted her to say *we? We'd* love that?

"What about the cat?"

He frowned at her. "Cat?"

"The cat under your porch and her kittens. Who's watching out for them?"

"Oh. That cat." He slid his hand up and down her arm. "They're living in my trailer now. I left the door open one afternoon and next thing I knew, they'd moved in. Abby's taking care of them while I'm gone.''

He felt her smile against his chest and snuggle closer.

"Lucian?"

"Yeah?"

There was a long pause before she finally lifted her gaze to his. "You don't have to get a hotel."

His heart jumped. He could see the uncertainty in her eyes. They were being so damn cautious, circling around each other. Why couldn't they just say what they were thinking? he wondered.

"You have a guest room?"

Her hands, soft and warm and smooth, moved down his sides. "No."

"A big sofa?"

"Only five feet."

"Why, Mrs. Sinclair," he drawled, "are you suggesting that I sleep in your bed?"

Her eyelashes fluttered down and she blushed. "It's a big bed. And it would be convenient." Her blush deepened. "To be close to Emma, I mean."

"Well, we certainly want what's best for Emma now, don't we?" He smiled, felt as if his entire body were grinning with him. "What about Teresa?"

"We *are* married, you know," she said. "Though we may have to show her the license before she approves."

He brought his mouth close to hers. "You sure I won't be in the way?"

"I think that's kinda the idea, Lucian," she murmured, parting her lips.

"What about your Italian friend?" he asked, part of him teasing, part of him wanting to know.

"Italian friend?"

"The man you were talking to earlier in the suit. Armani, gold cuff links. Will he be upset if I'm there?"

She opened her eyes. "Antonio Barducci? He's a columnist with *New York Sophisticate*."

"He was whispering in your ear." Lucian nibbled on her earlobe. "I didn't like it."

Her laughter started somewhere deep in her chest, then rose like bubbles in champagne. Frowning, he lifted his head. "What's so funny?"

"He—" she turned her head into the pillow, then rolled out from under him. "He asked me if you were available. He said you were *bellissimo*."

Heat flashed up Lucian's neck. "That's not funny."

She sat on the edge of the bed, still laughing. "It's hysterical."

"The hell it is," he muttered irritably. "What did you tell him?"

"I gave him your phone number."

"What!"

"I'm kidding." She reached for his shirt and tugged it on. "I told him you were my husband and to back off."

He heaved a sigh of relief. "Good."

She glanced over her shoulder at him and grinned. "I told him I thought you were *bellissimo,* too."

"Yeah?" He grinned back at her, then fluffed the pillows and patted the bed. "Come back here and say that again. It turned me on."

She bounced off the bed.

"Hey. Where are you going?"

She disappeared through the door before he even had a chance to admire those incredible legs of hers. Frowning, he tossed the sheet off and started to follow.

When she came back through the doorway, his heart leaped in his throat, then every drop of blood above his waist went south. She sauntered toward him, his unbuttoned shirt showing more than a glimpse of her long, naked body. In one hand she held a bottle of champagne, in the other, the canister of whipped cream.

"I know something else that might turn you on." A smile touched her lips as she moved closer. "What do you think?"

He couldn't think at all, but it didn't matter. It wasn't a question that required a response with words.

For the next week, the New York fashion world buzzed over Raina's new line of lingerie. *Inventive, sexy* and *trendsetting* were just a few of the adjectives being bantered around in trade publications and newspapers. Not to mention word-of-mouth. Orders were pouring in, and the phones at her office never stopped. Even now, as she rode up the elevator to her apartment, her ears still seemed to be ringing. She was thrilled by all the brouhaha, but exhausted at the same time.

Pretty much the same feelings she had toward Lucian.

They had gone back to her apartment together early the next morning after they'd made love that first night. Emma had still been asleep, and Lucian had stood over his daughter's crib, watching her, waiting anxiously for her to stir. At the first sign of movement, he'd picked her up and cuddled, then said, "Good morning, sweetheart," as if he'd been doing it her entire life.

Raina's chest ached at the sight of Emma's welcoming smile, the way she hugged her body close to Lucian's and put her head on his shoulder. At that moment Raina knew that if she hadn't already loved him, she would have fallen for him all over again right then and there.

But she did love him. She always had, she always would.

She'd hoped in the time they'd spent together that he might come to love her, too. But he'd never said the words to her she so desperately needed to hear. He seemed perfectly content with everything as it was. While she was gone at work, he spent his days with Emma.

The nights, Raina thought with a mixture of pleasure and pain, he spent with her, in her bed. She'd had so little sleep this week, she was running on sheer adrenaline. Not that she'd complained, she thought with a smile. If anything, she'd been the one who couldn't keep her hands off him. It had been an incredible, wild, thrilling week.

And it was about to come to an end.

Keys in her hand, she paused outside her apartment door, needing a moment to find her balance. She knew she shouldn't be upset with him because he hadn't offered more to her. She was the one who'd invited him into her home, into her bed. She hadn't asked for more, or anything at all in return. That would have required courage.

But the fact was, she wanted more. Needed more.

She'd enjoyed every minute of the time they'd spent together these past few days, but she wouldn't do this again. Couldn't go through the hurt every time he would have to leave.

They could be friends, they needed to be, for Emma's sake. But Raina knew now that she couldn't settle for anything less than a real marriage with Lucian. It wasn't enough for her to love him. She needed him to love her back.

She sighed, pressed her forehead to the doorjamb and closed her eyes. When the time was right, in a few months, maybe a year, she would file for divorce.

Sucking in a deep breath, she quietly opened her apartment door, saw Lucian playing "Itsy-Bitsy Spider" with Emma on the carpet in the living room.

Her heart ached at the sight of them, this six-foot-four man rippling his fingers and singing "down came the rain" to his tiny daughter.

"Something smells good." She stepped inside and sniffed the air. Teresa's spaghetti sauce, Raina was certain. Forcing a smile, she closed the door behind her. "Hello, sweetheart."

Lucian looked up at Raina's greeting. The endearment wasn't for him, of course, it was for Emma. Still, that single word, spoken with such tenderness and pleasure, brought a strange hitch in his chest. He smiled at her, then scooped Emma up in his arms and stood. "Give Mommy a kiss hello."

Raina kissed Emma's cheek, then nuzzled her neck, which brought a burst of giggles from the baby. When

Lucian bent to kiss Raina's neck, he felt her stiffen and move away.

"Have you eaten?" she asked.

She looked tired, he thought. And tense. He thought of a dozen ways to ease that tension. "Emma had some mashed rigatoni. She wanted to share, but I told her I was waiting for you."

Raina slipped her coat off and hung it up in the closet. There was a pause, a slight hesitation before she turned around.

"Something wrong?" he asked carefully.

"Bath time!"

Teresa came out of the bathroom, where Lucian could hear the water already running. He'd become fond of the tiny, silver-haired Greek nanny these past few days. She was a stern woman, all business, but her love not only for Emma, but for Raina, as well, was evident in the way she constantly fussed over them. It had taken him a day or two to get her to warm up to him, but he'd finally succeeded by bringing her a wedge of baklava from Nick's Greek Bakery across town. The next morning and every morning since, there'd been a fresh pot of coffee brewing for him when he'd come out of the bathroom. And whenever he got back from taking Emma on her walk, lunch would be waiting on the table. Yesterday she'd even made chocolate-chip cookies after she'd heard him mention to Raina that they were his favorite.

A terrific woman, he thought with a smile as he handed Emma over to the nanny.

"I'll come help," Raina offered, but Teresa waved her off, tickling Emma's belly with a stuffed terry-

cloth duck for the bath as they headed for the bathroom.

"I've never seen that duck before." Raina lifted a
brow as she looked at him. "Have you been out shop-
ping again?"

"I haven't got anything else to do while she's napping. And I bought something for you, too." Grinning, he pulled two tickets out of his shirt pocket.
"Dark Water. Friday night. Eight o'clock. You and
me."

He'd been anxious to see the expression on Raina's
face when he showed her the tickets. The play was
the hottest new thing on Broadway. He'd nearly had
to sell his soul and do back flips to get the seats with
only two days' notice.

"Thank you." She smiled weakly. "It's a wonderful thought."

Thank you? It's a wonderful thought? Hardly the
response he'd been expecting. He furrowed his brow,
watched her move into the kitchen and lift the lid off
the pot on the stove. Steam rose along with the rich,
spicy scent of tomatoes and herbs. She looked more
than tired, he thought. She looked exhausted.

She'd had a busy week since the show last week,
he reasoned. And she hadn't had much sleep at night,
either, which was definitely his fault.

He'd make sure she got to bed early tonight, he
told himself. To *sleep.*

He came up behind her, slid his hands up her arms.
"It's a wonderful thought, but?"

She leaned back against him for a moment, then
turned and stepped away. "But I can't go."

Something was wrong. Something more than long hours at work and lack of sleep.

Like a fist, an uneasiness settled in his gut. "You wanna tell me what's going on?"

"Lucian—" She hesitated, then drew in a long breath. "I've been offered a contract with Rossina Designs in Florence."

"Rossina Designs?" Though he'd never bought anything from the upscale clothing company, he'd certainly heard of them. Unless you lived in a cave, everyone had. "As in Florence, Italy?"

"Yes."

"Contracts are usually something to celebrate," he said evenly. "You wanna tell me why you look as if you just ran over a puppy?"

"The contract is for me to go to Florence and work with them there."

The fist in his gut tightened. "You're going to Italy? When?"

"Tomorrow."

"*Tomorrow?*"

"I'm sorry." Her voice shook slightly. "I know this is short notice. Everything has just happened so fast."

"I'd say that's a bit of an understatement." He told himself to be calm, then very carefully said, "All right. I can stick around here with Emma for a few more days until you get back."

She folded her arms tightly, as if she were cold, then closed her eyes. When she opened them again, she said, "Lucian, I'm taking Emma. We'll be gone for six months."

He went still, and the fist in his gut turned ice cold.

"You're going to Florence, *tomorrow,* for *six* months, and you're taking my daughter with you? Just like that?"

"It's an incredible opportunity that could mean a great deal for my business. I can't turn it down."

"Like hell you can't." He bit back the adjectives threatening to spill out. "You can do anything you want."

"I've worked hard for three years on my own to build a name for my designs." She looked directly at him, held her gaze steady with his. "Why would I say no to something like this?"

Why would she? he thought, clenching his jaw. She *had* worked hard to build her business and reputation in the fashion world, he'd learned that much from talking to her associates at the party. But *six* months?

"Six months will go by quickly," she said. "When we get back—"

"Dammit, Raina, you aren't going!" He swung away from her, raked a hand through his hair. "You can't just take Emma and leave like this. She's my daughter, and in case you've forgotten, we happen to be married."

"Signing a license and wearing rings doesn't make this a marriage," she said quietly. "We agreed to marry to give Emma your name. We also agreed that at some point our marriage would be dissolved. As far as I've seen, nothing's changed."

He could barely hear her words over the roar of blood rushing through his brain. Anger washed over him, and he struggled to keep his voice down. *Dammit!*

"Fine," he ground out. "Go to Florence. But leave Emma with me."

Shock registered on her face, but she quickly recovered. "Out of the question."

"Why? You'll be working all day. I'll take six months off. Callan and Gabe can run things for me, and I'll take care of Emma."

She advanced on him then, her lips pressed into a thin line. "Emma is my life. I love her. I would *never, ever,* leave her. She stays with me."

The fierce love that shone in Raina's narrowed eyes, the tone in her voice that resembled a lioness protecting her cub, took some of the heat out of Lucian's temper. In his gut he knew she was right, that Emma should stay with her, but his heart was telling him something different. He just didn't know exactly what.

"I love her, too," he said through gritted teeth. "Doesn't what I want count for anything here?"

"More than you know," she said softly. "You'll love her forever, Lucian. She's part of you and she always will be. Don't you know that?"

At the sound of Emma's splashing and laughter from the bathroom, they both turned.

It took every ounce of willpower he possessed not to yell, not to put his hands on Raina and shake her, then kiss her senseless and *make* her change her mind.

But he could see the determination in her eyes. She wouldn't change her mind. She was going. With Emma.

And there wasn't a damn thing he could do about it.

Jaw tight, lips pressed into a thin line, he turned

back to her. "I'm going to dress Emma and put her to bed. You eat."

He turned away from her, thankful that she didn't argue. After he dressed his daughter, after he rocked her to sleep and covered her with a blanket, then quietly crept out of her bedroom, he grabbed his jacket and headed for the front door.

He intended to find the closest bar and order a tall, stiff drink.

Or maybe two.

Twelve

With a diaper bag slung over one shoulder and tote bag on the other, Raina followed Teresa and a sleeping Emma through the sea of people in the noisy terminal. She always allowed plenty of time at the airport, and today, with short lines at the ticket counter, plus a thirty-minute delay on her flight, they still had an hour before their plane took off. Normally all that extra time would calm her, but today all she'd wanted to do was leave.

Except she *didn't* want to leave. She could hardly bear the thought of actually getting on that plane and leaving Lucian.

She swallowed back the sickness in her throat and moved with the river of people flowing through the corridors, felt as if she was surrounded by happy, smiling faces. Couples holding hands or walking arm in arm, excitement dancing in their eyes as they prepared to board their planes. A man and woman, obviously just reunited, stood by a money exchange machine and embraced, oblivious to the crowd around them. It was a tender scene, one that would make most people smile or feel warm inside.

It made Raina want to cry like a baby.

Maybe it wouldn't have been so bad if she'd at least been able to speak with Lucian before they'd left. If they hadn't argued last night. If he hadn't left as he had, angry and frustrated.

If he hadn't come in drunk as a skunk at 3:00 a.m.

She was certain he had no recollection of her helping him to the sofa, not an easy feat considering his size. But somehow she'd managed, then taken off his shoes as he'd curled up on the sofa.

She'd looked at him then, lying there so helpless, and she'd wanted desperately to cancel her trip. To forget the contract the designer had proposed, or at least offer to send Annelise in her place. Her assistant was eager and talented. Between fax, phone, computers and maybe one or two short trips to Florence, Raina could have made it work.

But the moment had passed quickly. If Lucian couldn't ask her to stay, if he couldn't say the words to her that she so badly needed to hear, there was no reason to stay. No reason to try.

I love you.

That was what she wanted, what she needed. He might be content to keep things as they were: a wedding ring but no commitment, sex but no love. She couldn't.

She wouldn't.

Not anymore.

Still, she wasn't sorry she married him. Emma would have her daddy's name, and no one would ever whisper or point fingers at her. She would know more love from Lucian and his family than Raina could ever have hoped for her daughter to have. Emma would always be safe.

But the pain of loving Lucian and not being loved in return would destroy her, Raina knew. She also knew that she would never love anyone again as much as she loved him. She could never come close.

She'd tried to wake him this morning, had called his name and shaken his arm, but he hadn't stirred. Not even when the doorbell had rung, or when the driver had carried their luggage out. Not even when she'd lightly kissed him on his forehead. She'd left a note on the kitchen counter, saying goodbye and giving him her hotel information and phone number in Florence, but she hadn't left him her flight information.

Maybe it was better this way, she thought. Better to leave the way she had, quietly. If he had wakened and they'd argued, it would only have been worse. More heartache, that was all she would have brought away with her.

If it were possible to have more, she thought, blinking back the threatening tears.

When Lucian woke he felt as if the Macy's Day Parade had set up its route directly inside his head. Crowds screamed, tubas blasted, bands marched right through the center of his brain. His mouth felt like cotton candy, minus the candy, and his stomach lurched like one of those giant blowup figures caught in the wind.

If he'd had a cork in his head, Lucian thought, there was no doubt it would blow off right about now.

Carefully he opened his eyes, groaned, then slammed them shut again.

The morning sun burned straight through his eyeballs, giving new meaning to the term "liquid fire." Pain bounced like pinballs inside his skull, complete with bells and whistles.

If he lived—and he wasn't so certain he wanted to—he never wanted to hear the term "race beers" again.

Still wearing the same clothes from last night, he unfolded his bent knees very, very slowly and sat, had to grip the side of the mattress to keep himself from falling flat on his face off the edge of the bed.

Not a bed, he realized as his eyes slitted open again.

The couch.

No wonder his body felt as if he'd been stuffed inside a washing machine and set on heavy-load cycle. His joints popped as he stretched, and the dull, heavy pounding inside his head turned needle sharp.

Stupid. Stupid. Stupid.

He had intended to cut the edge of his frustration, but he hadn't intended to drink as much as he had. He hadn't even ordered anything hard, as he'd originally intended. But one beer had led to another, and before he knew it, he'd been commiserating with several of the other patrons there and they'd all wanted to buy him drinks. Fortunately, a couple of his new-found pals had helped him back to the apartment, though he wasn't sure what time that had been.

He glanced at his wristwatch, waited a moment for the dial to come into focus. *Dammit.* It was almost eleven.

The apartment was quiet. Too quiet. And he knew. Knew that they'd already left.

He had no idea which airline or what time their flight was leaving. All she had said was afternoon.

Dammit, dammit, *dammit.*

The last morning he would have had to spend time with his daughter for six months and he blew it by lying around in a drunken stupor.

And Raina.

It was the last chance he had to see her for six months, too. He rubbed at the tightness in his chest and knew it had nothing to do with too many beers.

They were leaving today. Flying off to Florence.

He closed his eyes and hauled in a slow breath, then dragged his hands through his hair. Even that slight movement made his head pulsate. The only other time he'd ever woken up feeling like this was the morning after his accident and he'd found himself lying in a hospital bed. That hadn't been a great deal of fun, either.

Ironic, wasn't it, that both occasions revolved around Raina. He'd only wanted to go out and buy the woman some flowers, for God's sake, a few roses or—

His eyes flew open and he glanced up sharply, ignoring the pain that shot through his temple.

Flowers.

He'd gone out to buy her flowers. It had been too

early on a Sunday morning for the florist to be open, so he'd taken the back road leading to Sydney's restaurant, hoping that she'd have some extra roses. It had snowed the night before...the roads were slick. He'd been lost in thought, thinking about Raina...the truck slid on a patch of ice and then—

Nothing.

Dammit! He couldn't remember what happened after that. Blackness. Absolute, complete darkness.

He closed his eyes, pushed out every other thought and simply let his mind take him....

Gabe and Melanie's wedding...the sound of silverware clinking on champagne glasses. *To the bride and groom,* he could hear himself saying...

But he'd already remembered that little snippet of the wedding, Lucian thought in frustration. The toast he'd made to the bride and groom.

He forced himself to relax...saw himself standing in the back of the ballroom...Raina beside him...

Why don't I drive you back? I've got to take these presents over to the house, anyway.

At Gabe's house, brushing the snow off his jacket after the last present had been brought in....

Would you like some coffee?

Sure.

They'd stared at each other, only inches apart...and then she was in his arms, he was kissing her, both of them drunk, not from champagne, but each other.

Oh, God. He remembered. Not details, but most of it. Staggering up the stairs, struggling with clothes, the desperation to make love with her.

The morning after.

Be back in fifteen. Please don't leave.

He hadn't wanted her to go. He'd wanted her to stay. With him.

Just like now.

Panic filled him. How could this be happening twice?

I'm leaving for Florence Friday morning. I'll be gone six months.

Through the thick fog covering his brain, her words from last night came rushing back to him.

Why would I say no to something like this? she'd asked him and he hadn't had an answer.

Signing a license and wearing rings doesn't make this a marriage...as far as I've seen, nothing's changed.

Why would I say no to something like this...?

Nothing's changed....

His skull nearly broke in two at the sudden explosion of bells inside his head. The phone, he realized, and grimaced at the persistent shrieking.

The phone! It had to be Raina. It had to be!

He tripped over his feet, half stumbled, half crawled to the kitchen phone and snatched the receiver off its cradle.

"Raina!" he shouted into the phone. "Raina, is that you?"

"'Fraid not," Melanie said at the other end of the line. "Guess you'll just have to talk to me instead."

The call for her flight's departure brought Raina's head up from the game of peekaboo she'd been playing with Emma. Beside her, Teresa stood, then held her hands out to the baby, who smiled brightly and pumped her arms in excitement.

"Time to go, sweetheart," Raina said as she kissed her daughter, then handed her to Teresa.

With a sigh Raina gathered the diaper bag and her tote, then followed Teresa and Emma toward the gate entrance with all the other boarding passengers. Outside the tall, glass window, Raina saw their plane, heard the loud whir of its engine.

The finality of it, knowing that she was really leaving, made her chest ache.

Blinking back the threatening tears, she reached into her bag for their boarding passes, pulled them out and started to hand them to a pretty blond gate attendant—

"Raina! Stop!"

Her head jerked up at the frantic call.

"Please, stop, just stop!"

Her heart did stop.

Lucian.

He came running through the crowd of people, barreling his way through the bodies surrounding him, yelling her name.

Her heart kicked into high gear, hammering against her ribs. All she could do was stare as he came at her like a quarterback with a football.

"Lucian?"

Out of breath, he slammed to a stop in front of her. His face was flushed and unshaven, his hair spiked on the top, and he was still wearing the same wrinkled blue shirt and jeans he'd had on this morning. He smelled like strong coffee and peppermint.

"Raina," he gasped between breaths. "You can't leave."

"What are you doing here?" She wasn't certain

her knees would hold her, they were shaking so badly. "How did you know how to even find me?"

"Melanie," he said, still breathing heavy. "She called this morning. She knew. You can't leave, Raina. You can't."

Raina glanced around at all the faces staring curiously at them. Even Teresa watched, one brow lifted. "Lucian, we've been through this. Nothing's changed."

"Excuse me," the gate attendant said a bit impatiently, "are you coming through?"

"Yes." Raina held the tickets out.

"No." He snatched them away.

"Hey!" She narrowed a gaze at him. "Give those back to me."

He looked over at Teresa. "Teresa, please, just wait right there," he said, then took hold of Raina's shoulders and pulled her aside to let other passengers go by. "Raina, please, you've got to at least listen to me."

"You've got thirty seconds." Any longer than that, and she knew she'd crumble, that she'd say yes to anything as long as she could be with him.

"You're wrong."

Her heart sank. "You came all the way down here to tell me I'm wrong? Goodbye, Lucian."

She tried to pull away, but he tightened his hold. "Will you just listen to me? I came here to tell you that you're wrong about nothing changing. It *has* changed, dammit. Everything has changed."

She went still at the urgency in his voice and the desperation in his eyes. And there was something else, something she dared not even think...

"You were wrong when you said there was no reason for you to stay." His hands gentled on her arms, and his voice softened. "And you were wrong when you said our marriage was nothing more than a license and rings. You're wrong, Raina. There's every reason for you to stay."

"What, Lucian?" she heard her own breathless whisper. "What reason?"

"I love you."

The breath she'd been holding shuddered out. She looked into his eyes and it *was* there, what she'd thought she'd seen. She had to swallow the thickness in her throat before she could speak.

"You love me?"

"I've loved you from the moment I first laid eyes on you."

"You mean at the airport in Philadelphia?"

He shook his head. "No. I mean the *first* time."

"But you don't...you couldn't remember."

"I couldn't, until this morning. I'm still fuzzy on a lot, but the one thing I remember with clarity is the most important. I admit I resisted, that I even denied it to myself, but it's the truth, sweetheart. I fell head over heels in love with you at first sight. I didn't want you to leave after Gabe and Melanie's wedding. I wanted you to stay with me."

As worked up as he was, as frantic as he was, Raina was surprised that airport security hadn't already dragged him away. But it seemed as if everyone around them was simply watching, waiting with bated breath to see how this real-life drama would unfold.

She still wasn't sure herself.

"What are you saying, Lucian?" she asked carefully, needed to be very, very sure that she wasn't misunderstanding.

"Stay with me." He took her hand, brought it to his lips. "You and Emma. We can live anyplace you want. Bloomfield, New York, Florence. Timbuktu. I don't give a damn as long as you let me love you. As long as you give me a chance to make you love me, too."

Too staggered to speak, she stared at him. He didn't know? He couldn't see?

"Are you blind, Lucian?" she finally managed to say, then started to laugh. "You big idiot. Of course I love you!"

Relief poured through Lucian. *She loves me,* he thought, delirious with joy. Like the love-happy idiot he truly was, he gave a shout and picked her up. Her bags dropped to the ground, and he swung her around. Laughing, she wrapped her arms around his neck.

When he set her back down again, he kissed her, a long, deep, lingering kiss.

"Ah, excuse me," the gate attendant said awkwardly. Even she had a hopeful look on her face. "But we're going to have to close the gate. Are you staying?"

"If you can't stay," he said roughly, felt the words rip at his gut, "I'll catch the next flight. I can't be without you and Emma, I can't live without either one of you. Not even six hours, let alone six months. God, I need you both."

"You don't have to go anywhere, Lucian." She cupped his face in her hands. "I'm staying. Of course, I'm staying."

At the sound of scattered applause, Lucian glanced

up. Several women had wistful expressions on their faces, and a few of the men were grinning. Even Teresa had tears in her eyes. With a nod of approval, the nanny walked over and placed his sleeping daughter into his arms.

He had to swallow the tightness in his throat, was certain his heart was about to swell and burst with the love he felt for the child in his arms and the woman at his side.

"What about Florence?" he asked, afraid to give her an opportunity to change her mind, but knew that he had to. "What will happen if you don't go?"

"I'll have to make a lot of phone calls, but I can make it work," she said. "Looks like my assistant is going to get that trip to Italy she's always wanted."

"I can move to New York," he said firmly. "My brothers can take over my end of the business. I can sell the house once it's finished—"

"Sell our house?" She frowned and shook her head. "Not on your life. I've already got my office picked out, first bedroom on the upstairs right. Our daughter's bedroom will be across the hall."

"And the other two bedrooms?" He lifted a brow. "What do you suggest we do with those?"

"Well," she said, curving her lips, "it *would* be a shame to waste all that wonderful space, now wouldn't it?"

"Yeah, it would." He wondered how fast he could finish the house, if it were possible for his daughter to say her first word or take her first step in their new home together. He'd have help, he knew. Callan and Gabe and Reese, they'd all pull together for him. Together they could make it happen.

But the thought of his brothers also made him wince.

"Lord help me if my brothers ever catch wind of what I did here today," he said with a chuckle. "They would rib me ruthlessly for the rest of my life."

Amusement and love shone in Raina's deep-blue eyes as she slipped an arm through his and leaned over to kiss her daughter's cheek. "Just as long as we're around to see it."

"Oh, you're going to be around, all right." He deepened the kiss. "For the rest of my life, darlin'."

"You think you can remember that, Lucian?" She leaned toward him, pressed her lips lightly to his.

"I'll remember." He deepened the kiss and smiled. "Trust me, I'll remember."

* * * * *

Look for more Secrets!
Stories from Barbara McCauley in 2002.

THE FORTUNES OF TEXAS

invite you to meet

THE LOST HEIRS

Silhouette Desire's scintillating
new miniseries, featuring the beloved

FORTUNES OF TEXAS

and six of your favorite authors.

A Most Desirable M.D.—June 2001
by Anne Marie Winston (SD #1371)

The Pregnant Heiress—July 2001
by Eileen Wilks (SD #1378)

Baby of Fortune—August 2001
by Shirley Rogers (SD #1384)

Fortune's Secret Daughter—September 2001
by Barbara McCauley (SD #1390)

Her Boss's Baby—October 2001
by Cathleen Galitz (SD #1396)

Did You Say Twins?!—December 2001
by Maureen Child (SD #1408)

And be sure to watch for *Gifts of Fortune*,
Silhouette's exciting new single title,
on sale November 2001

*Don't miss these unforgettable romances…
available at your favorite retail outlet.*

Silhouette®
Where love comes alive™

July 2001
COWBOY FANTASY
#1375 by Ann Major

August 2001
HARD TO FORGET
#1381 by Annette Broadrick

September 2001
THE MILLIONAIRE COMES HOME
#1387 by Mary Lynn Baxter

October 2001
THE TAMING OF JACKSON CADE
#1393 by BJ James
Men of Belle Terre

November 2001
ROCKY AND THE SENATOR'S
DAUGHTER
#1399 by Dixie Browning

December 2001
A COWBOY'S PROMISE
#1405 by Anne McAllister
Code of the West

MAN OF THE MONTH

For over ten years Silhouette Desire has been
where love comes alive, with our passionate,
provocative and powerful heroes. These ultimately,
sexy irresistible men will tempt you to turn every
page in the upcoming **MAN OF THE MONTH**
love stories, written by your favorite authors.

Available at your favorite retail outlet.

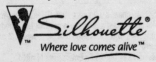

Silhouette®
Where love comes alive™

Visit Silhouette at www.eHarlequin.com   SDMOM01-2

CALL THE ONES YOU LOVE OVER THE HOLIDAYS!

Save $25 off future book purchases when you buy any four Harlequin® or Silhouette® books in October, November and December 2001,

PLUS

receive a phone card good for 15 minutes of long-distance calls to anyone you want in North America!

WHAT AN INCREDIBLE DEAL!

Just fill out this form and attach 4 proofs of purchase (cash register receipts) from October, November and December 2001 books, and Harlequin Books will send you a coupon booklet worth a total savings of $25 off future purchases of Harlequin® and Silhouette® books, AND a 15-minute phone card to call the ones you love, anywhere in North America.

Please send this form, along with your cash register receipts as proofs of purchase, to:
In the USA: Harlequin Books, P.O. Box 9057, Buffalo, NY 14269-9057
In Canada: Harlequin Books, P.O. Box 622, Fort Erie, Ontario L2A 5X3
Cash register receipts must be dated no later than December 31, 2001.
Limit of 1 coupon booklet and phone card per household.
Please allow 4-6 weeks for delivery.

**I accept your offer! Enclosed are 4 proofs of purchase.
Please send me my coupon booklet
and a 15-minute phone card:**

Name: _____

Address: _____ City: _____

State/Prov.: _____ Zip/Postal Code: _____

Account Number (if available): _____

---

097 KJB DAGL
PHQ4013

THE
F RTUNES
OF TEXAS

invite you to a memorable Christmas celebration in

Gifts of
F RTUNE

Patriarch Ryan Fortune has met death head-on and now he has a special gift for each of the four honorable individuals who stood by him in his hour of need. This holiday collection contains stories by three of your most beloved authors.

THE HOLIDAY HEIR
by Barbara Boswell

THE CHRISTMAS HOUSE
by Jennifer Greene

MAGGIE'S MIRACLE
by Jackie Merritt

And be sure to watch for **Did You Say Twins?!** by Maureen Child, the exciting conclusion to the *Fortunes of Texas: The Lost Heirs* miniseries, coming only to Silhouette Desire in December 2001.

Don't miss these unforgettable romances... available at your favorite retail outlet.

Silhouette®
Where love comes alive™

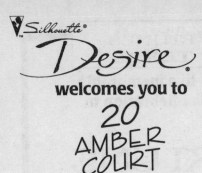